WANDERER

SAILOR

REBEL

FOOL

The God Who Rescues

WANDERER

SAILOR

REBEL

FOOL

The God Who Rescues

Scott R Harpole

TABLE OF CONTENTS

Look, we bless and honor the memory
of those who persevered under hardship.
Remember how Job endured and how the
Lord orchestrated the triumph of his final
circumstances as a grand display of
His mercy and compassion.

James 5:11 (VOICE)

THE PROBLEM

When your terror comes like a storm,
and your destruction comes like a whirlwind,
when distress and anguish come upon you.

Proverbs 1:27 (NKJV)

A DEADLY STORM

Reiko was dead and no one knew why.

How is it that a single moment from your childhood can anchor itself and remain perfectly clear in your mind for your entire life? I have forgotten thousands of moments since then, but this one stays with me.

The day was unremarkable. It could've been summer. Or was it a Saturday? I know it was the early 70s, and I know I was home from school. I was playing on the floor in the kitchen when my mom answered the phone. She had been talking and singing all morning, but suddenly her words were slow and deliberate. I don't know what was said to her, but there was something terrible about her reaction. I can't remember her words, but I can still see her face. Her expression transformed from sunny and relaxed to cloudy and stunned.

When I saw tears roll down Mama's cheeks, the little game I had been playing fell to the ground. She didn't try to stop them or even wipe them away; she was so intent on listening. I ran to hug her, to make it better, though I did not understand why she was crying.

I wouldn't fully understand until much later.

Part of our family was gone.

Reiko had been my mom's close friend. She and her husband, Sid, were like family to us. It was always Mom and Reiko, Dad and Sid. They were over at our house often, and we were with them all the time, especially my little brother. This childless couple practically adopted him. They watched him at their house and held him at church. Before he was born, Reiko had asked my mother to pray with her that God would give her a baby. So when Mom got pregnant with my brother, Reiko semi-jokingly said that God put the baby in the wrong mother.

Years later, Mom told me about Reiko's first prayer, the one that led to her conversion. After being raised in Buddhism and then marrying a Christian, she wanted to know which God was the true God. She asked the God of the Bible to show her if he was real. And he did just that. One night, while sitting on a church pew, God showed her a vision of himself in the church above the platform. Her life was transformed that night, and from then on she was determined to tell everyone about Jesus.

That's why she bought the pamphlets.

It wasn't until much later in life that I heard the full story. Reiko had been driving on a busy St. Louis interstate, ready to witness to others with her brand-new

4

Bible study materials in the passenger seat when her car inexplicably angled across the median into oncoming traffic. There were no skid marks, no evidence that anyone had crashed into her. She collided with a huge truck at full speed and was pronounced dead at the scene. It was assumed that she'd had a heart attack, maybe even died before impact.

The details eluded us, but one thing was certain: Our precious family friend, Reiko, lost her life that day.

I'm unsure who babysat us kids, but I do know our parents stood in the hospital and mourned with Sid. They supported each other, they cried together. They prayed to God for help.

Words fail in those situations. What can you do in a time like that except hold on to each other and the Lord?

Why do I so clearly remember that one moment in the kitchen from fifty years ago? Was it the change in my mother's face? The way happiness and peace were sucked from the little house as fear and pain rushed in?

This was a sudden Distress, a hurricane of the heart. It was a spiritual explosion for her husband and the church family she left behind. One question persisted: "Why?" It's a question still unanswered. Why would this happen to her? Why would this happen to us?

She was a sweet, godly lady who helped others.

She was doing good things for God.

She was on her way to witness.

And then she was gone.

Trust in, lean on, rely on,
and have confidence in Him at all times,
you people; pour out your hearts before Him.
God is a refuge for us (a fortress and a high tower).
Selah [pause, and calmly think of that]!

Psalm 62:8 (AMPC)

DRY PLACES

The funeral was quickly over.

Everyone who'd known Reiko struggled with questions before, during, and after the service. But I wonder how many people also struggled with their faith beyond that day. It's normal to question God or even life itself during The Storm. But at what point do questions usher in the doubt that begins to erode faith? Would Sid continue to follow God? What about my parents, how would they react? Would this become a point in their lives in which they would choose to turn away from God? Would something like this cause them to step back? Would they forfeit their faith and trust, or would they rush to the Lord, holding tightly to him in their pain?

The ceremony was over, but the grief stayed around. It always does.

There's no way to measure the full impact of a Distress like The Storm. Grief isn't a puzzle to solve, and there's no magic key to heal from it, no matter how long or hard we search. It's a feeling you carry. And sometimes it can be so heavy that you can't do it alone. Christians are not exempt from pain. Unstoppable destruction can happen in the life of any believer. Yes, God can still The Storm, but he may also choose to take you *through* The Storm. It's difficult to overstate the importance of maintaining your trust in God in times of Distress.

Your life before The Storm is like traveling down a smooth highway. There are only a few exits, and you know where you want to go. Going through The Storm can feel like circling the East Longmeadow rotary in Massachusetts. There are no clear instructions, and seven roads converge, weaving in and out of the intersection. You must be very careful what exit you choose when you circle that rotary. The wrong turn will spin you out on a different road you can't easily get off of, sending you several miles in the wrong direction before you can turn around and try again.

Just like on the rotary, Distress can spin your life around, confuse your mind, and devastate your soul. It's easy to slip and lose your foothold before you've even realized it's happening. Often, counselors will encourage people who are grieving to avoid making major decisions. Many times, people unintentionally walk away from God during times of grief. Others may stay on the path but become cold due to heartache and disappointment.

Think about the generations to come after you.

One day they will be grateful that you held onto the Lord in your Distress. I am grateful that my parents did. My life is a living testimony that my parents refused to turn away from the Lord even when facing loss and encountering questions they could not answer.

As a child, I could not have grasped how pivotal the weathering of that Storm was for my parents. Pivotal for their three children and for their future ministry. Their decisions while trying to survive The Storm would impact thousands of people for years to come. They could not have imagined that in less than five years they would become pastors. That there would be a little country church that needed them. They didn't know that five churches would be born out of that one congregation. They didn't know that my brother and I would preach our first sermons there behind an old wooden pulpit. That I would meet my wife in that church. That my best memories would be made there.

What if they had turned away from God in those trying moments?

I don't know if my brother would be pastoring today.

I wonder where my sister would be.

I doubt this book would've been written.

If our parents hadn't chosen to cling to God during that Storm, I don't know how any of our lives would've turned out.

*O give thanks unto the LORD, for he is good:
for his mercy endureth for ever. Let the
redeemed of the LORD say so, whom he
hath redeemed from the hand of the
enemy; and gathered them out of the
lands, from the east, and from the west,
from the north, and from the south.*

Psalm 107:1–3

*Now these are Your servants and Your
people, whom You have redeemed by Your
great power, and by Your strong hand.*

Nehemiah 1:10 (NKJV)

REDEEMED FROM BABYLON

The Storm my parents experienced is an example of a Distress we see outlined in Psalm 107. This Psalm is not directed to the unbeliever, but to the Redeemed who are in Distress. It concludes the historical contrasts we see in Psalms 105 and 106, creating a trilogy of sorts.

Psalm 105 tells what God did: He created the people of Israel, took them from famine to prosperity in Egypt, brought plagues on Egypt and set Israel free, did great miracles among them, and brought them to the edge of the Promised Land.

Psalm 106 tells what the people did: They believed and were delivered from Egypt, but then they grew rebellious, erected the calf idol, disbelieved, were struck by plagues, and even made pagan sacrifices of their children. God handed them over to enemy oppressors, and Israel cried out for salvation.

Psalm 107 lays out their eventual return from exile, when The Redeemed were gathered from strange lands and finally traveled back home to the Promised Land.

God orchestrated a prison break for the generation living captive in Babylon. They didn't decide to be in captivity; they were born there. No one's strength, ideas, or ingenuity could break them out of the mess their ancestors had gotten them into. Only the hand of God could deliver them.

Verse 2 is a reminder of who we are in him—The Redeemed people he has gathered out of the hand of the enemy:

> Let the redeemed of the LORD say so, whom he hath redeemed from the hand of the enemy.
> (Psalm 107:2)

We are The Redeemed, the people he gathered and continues to gather from the hand of the enemy and from every point around the compass rose.

We are humbly thankful to be The Redeemed. But it isn't a title to boast about. It's not shameful by any means, but neither is it something to take personal pride in. We are not The Redeemed due to any action of our own. In fact, it's often our own actions that cause us to need redemption. "'Not by might nor by power, but by My Spirit,' says the LORD of hosts" (Zechariah 4:6b, NKJV).

The message of God's tender mercy and lovingkindness in Psalm 107 can literally save us from destruction. How? It can pull us out of the pit in our own minds and spirits. It has the power to turn our focus away from our personal list of impossible problems and free us to see the King of Glory. It enables us to experience Psalm 24:7 (NKJV), "Lift up your heads, O you gates! And be lifted up, you everlasting doors! And the King of glory shall come in."

God's Word provides the essential antidote for every problem. Its heavenly message in various applications brings us out from the pit and into his presence.

This book is an amplification of Psalm 107, with its intricate characters revealing God's message to us, The Redeemed. Investigating this psalm can help us clearly see where we are, how we got here, and how to get out. My prayer is that throughout this book God will reveal life-changing insights to you.

*When you are in distress, and all these
things come upon you in the latter days,
when you turn to the LORD your God and
obey His voice. (For the LORD your God is
a merciful God), He will not forsake you
nor destroy you, nor forget the covenant of
your fathers which He swore to them.*

Deuteronomy 4:30–31 (NKJV)

FOUR DISTRESSES

Psalm 107 is a message from God to his children, an instructional guide containing treasures that apply to every person who believes in him. You can tell this is a mystery to most Christians by their reaction to God when they encounter serious trouble, yet it's urgently needed by everyone who loves him.

The 3,000-year-old stories found in this psalm give us a crucial understanding of how to process the Distresses we encounter. In our lifetimes, we either have faced or will face one or more of these.

Distresses come into every life. Job said that man is of few days and full of trouble. (Job 14:1) It is impossible to go through this life unscathed by Distress. We live in a world of trouble and pain. The important truth from the story of Job, as well as that of my parents, is that it matters how we respond to Distress.

Distresses don't last forever. Solomon said there is a season to everything (Ecclesiastes 3:1). My favorite short phrase from the Bible is "and it came to pass." It's used nearly four hundred times, and it assures us that things are always changing. This means that every situation, trouble, or difficulty will eventually be over, whether in this life or the next.

Distress can bring frustration, endless questions, and pain. In the physical, it is impossible to be hit by a hurricane or cyclone and remain unaffected. I am grateful that most of our lives are not lived in a tornado. We do go through turmoil, but I'll put emphasis on the word through. Talk to enough Christians, and you'll find that everyone who follows Jesus still goes through Distresses.

Distresses can come from different directions: from without or within, from our fault, from their fault, from nobody's fault. The answer to weathering any of the Distresses we encounter in life can be found in this psalm, especially if we understand who it was written for and why.

No one desires to experience a life-threatening situation, a soul-extinguishing heartache, or a deep disappointment, but these troubles are an inevitable part of life on earth. Jesus plainly told us that in this world we will have trouble (John 16:33; the word tribulation in this verse means pressure or trouble). Yet the moment many Christians enter those painful and bewildering moments, they become distant from God, and their first love for him gets colder.

This psalm contains an eye-opening word picture that illustrates four Distresses: Wandering, Storms,

Rebellion, and Foolishness. Each of these Distresses is illustrated by a different character and setting.

You might be surprised to find what you have in common with a wilderness Wanderer, a grizzled Sailor, an incarcerated Rebel, or a dying Fool. It's impossible to avoid troubling situations like the ones these characters experienced.

In this book, we will do a deep dive to examine the painful stories of these four characters in their Distress. We'll find clues about why troubles happened to each of them, descriptions of their troubles, how they cried out to be rescued, and how God delivered them.

I'm approaching these characters differently than their order in the psalm. From the perspective of the cause of their Distress, we find that The Wanderer and The Sailor both portray Distresses that happen to us. No one can evade The Wilderness or outrun The Storm. Conversely, The Rebel and The Fool depict Distresses we bring on ourselves. These are The Prisons and Sickbeds we find ourselves in as a consequence of our own foolish or rebellious actions.

All four characters in Psalm 107 needed rescue from some version of Distress.

The Wanderer was lost in The Wilderness.

The Sailor was fighting for survival in The Storm.

The Rebel was on the floor in pain behind The Prison doors.

The Fool was lying in The Sickbed, unable to eat and near death.

Each character reached a point where they were in a life-threatening situation and cried out to God. If God did not respond to their cry, they would have been lost. They'd reached the end of their rope with no one who could help them. They desperately needed God's help.

At one point or another over my lifetime, I have personally identified with all four characters. Study this psalm with me to understand the Distresses we face and how they faced theirs. This is information that God wants us to know. When faced with Distress, the choices we make are critical.

Sometimes we relate to The Wanderer, disconnected from people and without direction. We don't see how God can put us on the right path and give us a place of connection. We need not give up in The Wilderness. We can be assured that God has direction and a plan for our lives, even if it seems impossible or farfetched.

Sometimes we are The Sailor, attempting to survive while The Storm rages and our world is under attack. This is when we hold on tight to God. He is the only source of peace. We trust that God can lead us out of The Storm and calm the wind and the waves. We may have currently lost our stability and sense of direction, but we trust that if we hold onto God, we'll be alright.

Sometimes we see ourselves in The Rebel, chained by depression, held in a Prison of our own making. This is the moment we need God to set us free. We believe God has power and ability far greater than any earthly heroes. We may feel only agony as we sit in darkness now, but we are confident that God will bring us out of the dark and into the precious light.

Sometimes we have been The Fool, sick unto death in spirit, mind, or body because of our own sin. We need faith greater than we can possess of ourselves. But when we put our faith in God, not in ourselves or other people, we remember that he can bring us out of this Distress. We know that God is the only one who can heal. One way or another, in this life or the next, God will deliver us from death.

What is the Lord ready to do today? The Bible says he is ready to forgive. He is poised to take action. "For thou, Lord, art good, and ready to forgive; and plenteous in mercy unto all them that call upon thee" (Psalm 86:5).

This book is directed to those who love the Lord. It is a cry from God's heart to those who attempt to follow him, even when they get lost along the way. It is to those who call themselves his disciples and to those who wish they could. God gave us this psalm to understand his heart. He wants us to see how he reaches out to hurting people.

I'm thankful for the message of Psalm 107, an allegory with application for every Christian. We see God ready to forgive each character, ready to hear their cry, ready to rescue them from destruction. And he's ready to do the same for us. God proves through these four stories that he is both willing and able to rescue people in every type of Distress known to mankind.

No matter the Distress, or how we may have gotten in it, this story is for us.

They wandered in the wilderness in a solitary way; they found no city to dwell in. Hungry and thirsty, their soul fainted in them. Then they cried unto the LORD in their trouble, and he delivered them out of their distresses. And he led them forth by the right way, that they might go to a city of habitation. Oh that men would praise the LORD for his goodness, and for his wonderful works to the children of men! For he satisfieth the longing soul, and filleth the hungry soul with goodness.

Psalm 107:4–9

THE WANDERER

And the Lord spoke to me, saying:
"You have skirted this mountain
long enough; turn northward."

Deuteronomy 2:2–3 (NKJV)

WANDERING

THE WANDERER

My wife and I were both born in Babylon. It's the only home we'd ever known. Along with many other Jewish families, we lived in a section of the big city that the Babylonians called Judahtown. Of course, there are dangers in a big city—soldiers to avoid, certain areas known for crime, and the sheer number of unknown people traveling through. Along with the soldiers, merchants, and visitors from all over the map, there was an undercurrent of tension between our people and the Babylonians that added a continual challenge to the daily grind. But providing for my wife and children was my priority, and overall, it was a wonderful place to be.

Our house was small, but the view of the city from the rooftop terrace made it feel much larger. At night after the kids were asleep, we would enjoy the cool breezes, watching the stars and listening to the sounds of the city. It was noisy, but the buzz it created was comforting. Back then, I couldn't imagine going to sleep without it.

But now. . .now it's different. I am wandering.

Neither lost nor found. I'm somewhere in the middle.

My wife heard the news while I was at work. I came home, wrung out after a trying day, looking forward to the peace of my rooftop terrace. Her eyes lit up in excitement with the news handed down from King Cyrus: We were free to go home. Home to Jerusalem.

At first, I refused. I just couldn't see how it would work.

"You want us to go 'home'? *This* is our home. Our life is here. Don't you love being on the roof? Tending your garden? You like discovering new things at the market. There won't be a market in the wilderness. And the one in Jerusalem won't be anything like what you're used to here. And what about our family? You talk to your sisters almost every day. What about my parents? They'd have to stay here. Do you think they could walk the two thousand miles with us? We'd be out there walking for at least four months, maybe five."

Right then too many chores vied for our attention, and too many questions were accumulating. So we fell into our normal evening routine. She waited until we got the kids in bed and retired to the rooftop before bringing up the topic again.

We looked at the stars. They always reminded me of the promise given to our Father Abraham about his children being as numerous as the stars in the heavens. But hadn't God also promised that those children would one day return home?

If I was being honest with myself, I could admit I felt the same way my wife did. Even though I was born and raised here in the city, I had always longed to see my ancestral home, Jerusalem. I could imagine being with the people of God, walking into our own city during a festival. I could hear the shouts of joy, the blast of the shofar echoing over the crowd. There was something compelling about the thought of returning to the home we were promised, but something reassuring about the stability we had established here.

"We'll need a donkey." She turned toward me, waiting.

I raised my eyebrows.

"And to learn how to pack a tent. What foods will keep or spoil. How to care for the children and the animals. . . ."

I sighed.

She grinned.

". . . I'm going to complain about the packing."

After talking for hours that night, we fell asleep on the rooftop. There were so many things we didn't know about taking such a long journey, especially with small children. We would have to learn what to buy, what to bring, what to leave behind. Everything we couldn't bring with us would be sold, including this house.

I prayed that Yahweh would honor our commitment.

This would not be easy, but our hearts were already in Jerusalem.

*And she wandered on [aimlessly] and lost
her way in the wilderness of Beersheba.*

Genesis 21:14b (AMPC)

RETURN HOME

THE WANDERER

After our decision to go to Jerusalem, we felt conflicting emotions: eagerness to be on our way, concern about all we needed to do before we left, and sadness at what we would leave behind. Everything we knew had to change.

Thinking about how to pack everything we needed to take filled us with trepidation. Our apprehension, while mixed with excitement, was also tinged with sadness at leaving our furniture, our friends, and especially our family. This would be a once-in-a-lifetime journey. We would never come back to our little Judahtown again. We could only keep those we loved in our minds as memories.

Not everyone was excited about our decision. Thousands of Jews leaving the workforce all at once impacted every part of the city. Those I worked with weren't happy to see me leave, but they understood. My wife and I both had friends and family who did their best to talk us out of going. Some said we'd regret it. "What if you die in the wilderness?" they asked. "What if your children are killed?" They urged us not to sell everything because we'd have nothing left to come back to.

They forgot that we wouldn't be traveling alone, and I did not believe any of my family would die. I think the truth was that they didn't want to leave the comfort of the city and were feeling conflicted that they'd chosen to not go with us.

The heaviness of last goodbyes was crushing. How do you hug your mom and dad for the last time? They had cried and held us close, especially the children. Until then I had refused to cry. But on that last day, I hugged and kissed them, then turned to walk away. When I looked back at them standing in their small doorway, I broke down and cried. One of my wife's sisters and several cousins stayed behind, so at least our parents wouldn't be alone and would have some family with them. But it still broke my heart.

Our bundle of possessions on that cart looked disproportionately tiny. How could everything we own be bound up behind a single donkey?

Yes, this was going to be hard. Hard but good.

It took a few days to find a rhythm. We would walk for most of the day until it was time to set up camp. My hands chaffed and bled at first, unused to the intensity of tying ropes, pulling the tent taut, getting water, hauling it back to camp—things we took for granted in the city. The tear down and set up of camp every morning and evening was demanding, but it was a welcome break from the endless walking. We passed the time by discussing the city of Jerusalem, the promises of God, and the most strategic way to rebuild the Temple. It kept us going with our heads held high and hope in our hearts. Sometimes we played games with the children: word games, quoting verses from the Torah, asking who could find a hawk in the sky or a snake along the ground.

Nights in the city were a constant buzz of predictable noise, something I hadn't realized I would miss. The silence of the wilderness almost felt loud, and each call of a bird or gust of wind echoed even louder because of it. In the beginning the nights were so full of strange sounds that I struggled to fall asleep. Over time, though, the rustling wind mixed itself with the cries of the various animals, and the rhythm of it soon became a comforting serenade that carried the quiet words floating from nearby tents like a lullaby.

Two or three months into our journey, we had become experienced, even practiced, travelers. When you're traveling, there were some things you have to live with. Dirt. Smells of unwashed bodies. And the people. Thousands of people were all around us, walking with us, talking with each other, fussing over silly things. I was thankful for the other travelers because it meant there were more people working together to find each well along the path for fresh water. Usually for meals, we had bread, grains, sometimes a stew. I often wished for meat, but that was a luxury in the wilderness. Nomadic life—even if temporary—was not easy, and nobody loved it. But the destination made it all worthwhile.

Eventually, this routine became our new normal. The dust and dirt. The hard work. The daily grind of endless walking and of guiding my family and the donkey. We were in transit and we lived like it. There was no planting of gardens, no working a daily job, no relaxing with the family. I was surprised by how much the lack of those things weighed and wore on us all. We reminded each other that this was just a season. There would be time to build a new life and to rest when we reached Jerusalem.

Yet I still couldn't think about our family who had remained behind without the knife-like pain of the loss slicing my gut. Missing them was that visceral. I constantly worked to redirect my mind and focus on where we were going rather than what we were leaving.

Underneath all the daily difficulty, the endless walking, and missing those we left behind was a depth of excitement that would sometimes poke through the surface of the drudgery. Now and then I would catch my wife smiling while she was busy cleaning something or brushing our daughter's hair.

Once, I asked why she was so happy.

"We are *doing* this," she said. "We are going home."

I laughed and shook my head. But I knew she was right.

We were going to the city of God.

Now a certain man found him, and
there he was, wandering in the field.

Genesis 37:15a (NKJV)

DIRECTIONLESS

THE WANDERER

The days grew unbearably hot, and we began shifting our routine to avoid the worst of the scorching sun. We soon turned to sleeping when the sun was the highest and walking in the cool of the early mornings and evenings instead. There were definite benefits to walking after the sun had gone down or barely come up. Little breezes and low heat made it more comfortable to travel.

But there were things to beware of at night.

It was no secret that bands of thieves preyed upon caravans like ours. And wild beasts roamed the wilderness for their own kind of prey. So we walked under the stars with heightened senses. Alert and ever watchful, we continually checked the terrain in all directions.

Sure, we were with a lot of people, but ultimately our caravan of travelers had no structured formation, and we were each responsible for our own families. Sometimes a family would be in the middle of the pack, while other times they would drop toward the rear. If a child was sick or a donkey was limping, the problem would have to be addressed before moving on. We all tried to stay together for community and safety, but it wasn't uncommon for a family to have to drop back temporarily and rejoin the group again later.

When we first lost sight of the largest part of the group, we weren't alarmed. It wasn't until farther into a particularly long stretch of not seeing anyone that we realized we might have gone off course. I didn't think we were lost, but I wasn't sure where we were either. The rising and setting of the sun had guided us. So I figured that if we continued west, away from the rising sun, we'd be heading in the right direction.

But where exactly were we? Where was the nearest well? And how could this happen to us? I had planned this trip so carefully. I had thought through every possibility. But now here we were, alone in the wilderness. We were no longer heading to Jerusalem, no longer led by visions of a new life in a city we longed to know. Suddenly, we were simply trying to survive.

The kids didn't know. They asked where some of their friends were, and we told them they were up ahead. That was true, though I didn't know which direction up ahead.

Water became scarce. The food I had complained about only weeks ago was being stretched thin. One of the hardest parts was when the children complained. My wife tried to comfort them, but it was becoming increasingly difficult to satisfy their growing hunger and thirst.

By this point we were basically walking blind—pushing forward every day, but without clear direction. I felt dead inside. Was I leading my children to their deaths? Next week, next month, next year, would we still be wandering around, lost in the wilderness? I don't know how we kept going. A city with people we loved awaited us at the other end of this journey, but I couldn't get us there. I did not know what to do or how to fix it.

Frustration gripped and squeezed my chest. Getting through each day was a struggle. I tried to keep it to myself and not burden my family, but the worry and uncertainty weighed heavily on my shoulders. I was like a dead man walking. I knew I had to keep going, but I was unsure of every step. *Oh God, have mercy on me! Get me back on the right path.*

We finally found a well, but no one else was there, and I still didn't know where we were. That night when the children fell asleep, my wife and I talked freely.

"What are we going to do?" It was not the first time either of us had asked that question.

"No matter what, we are not turning back." I didn't want to voice the fact that I truly didn't know what to do, so I started off with what I *did* know. "If we keep going west long enough, we will surely find somebody. . .or something that will confirm we're headed in the right direction."

She just looked at me.

It *had* sounded weak, even as I said it. But what else was I supposed to say?

I decided to go with *the truth*. I held her close and confessed it. "I don't know, Honey. I truly don't know." Admitting it gave me more courage than denying it had. Somehow, it seemed to reassure her too. Perhaps facing the fact that you're wandering brings more hope than avoiding hard truth.

For the moment, it was enough.

As we lay there trying to sleep, I worked things over in my mind. This was not how it was supposed to be. *God have mercy on my soul.* We thought we were doing the right thing, trying to get to God's city. Why were we so lost? It wasn't like we were disobeying the Lord or refusing to listen to him. We were following *his* promise. We sold everything to make this journey. We left precious family and friends—the most important things we had in this world. We even gave up our sweet little house. Why would God allow us to wander around lost and confused?

We used to smile and encourage one another by reminding ourselves of our purpose, but we no longer even had that. Our way was one of cloudiness, not clarity. When the body becomes exhausted, the spirit sinks. How much more so the mind? We began to walk more slowly, making less progress every day. What good does it do to hurry when there is no certainty in the direction? Who can keep up courage when utter exhaustion threatens to take you to the ground with each step?

The worry tended to surface at night when the work was done and we finally sat around the fire. My wife laid her head on my shoulder, and I ran my hand over her hair, as much for my comfort as for hers.

"I miss living in the city," was her new refrain. She had lost her resolve. "I want to see the other women, and houses, and the market."

"I know, honey."

"I don't want to travel anymore. I want to settle down and never move again. I miss our couch on the rooftop. I miss our garden."

"I know, sweetheart. I know."

The only thing worse than hearing the complaints of the children was seeing the misery of my wife. She's my heart. When she began to cry and shake in my arms, I felt that I was losing all ability to carry on.

Yet I still figured I could fix this mess. If I could only find a landmark or something, anything, to get my bearings. Then I would be able to chart our direction.

I tried to keep a positive mindset for the kids. I think it helped us all, really. Often I started the day by saying, "We are going to have a good day today!" Then I kept them occupied by challenging them: "Tell me if you see anything important that I might miss." Or I gave them a specific task: "Keep your eyes out for anything made by people—like a well, or tower, or even a pile of rocks." They enjoyed the game, and I had extra eyes on the terrain. It helped us feel hopeful for a while, but then hours passed by with only wilderness scrub and nothing human to be found. And my spirit slipped back into hopelessness.

Tonight was no different, except this time I

staggered to get the tent set up before the moon replaced the sun. I fell asleep, too weary to even cry.

What am I going to do? That's been *my* refrain. I don't have a pathway to get out of this. I only know how to push forward. Get up, every day, and walk.

We are wandering in the wilderness. The truth is that we are lost, though we continue trying to go the right way. We feel alone, despite knowing that God still loves us and is with us.

Directionless. Lonely. Afraid. Dead inside.

We need someone who can lead us out of our stupor. If only there were a clear path, a solid marker, to show me exactly which way to go. I wish with all my heart for a Guide who could take us to the City of David, to show me the right way, to make clear to me the path that leads out of this death into life.

The Wanderer's Prayer

Lord, lead me in the way you want me to go. I surrender my demands, my expectations for how this should work out. I lay my complaints on the ground and my frustrations at the altar of my relationship with you. Lord, be my guide. I will follow you through the back roads if that's what you decide, over rough terrain if you want, or through valleys with stops and starts if that's what you think is best for me. In the midst of enemies and uncertainty, I pray you would lead me in a level path and make Your way straight before my face. God, I would like to say that I'll never wander again, but if something happens and I veer from the good path, help me to quickly be restored

—Paraphrased from Psalm 5:8 and 27:11)

And [he] makes them wander
in a pathless wilderness.

Job 12:24b

WHO IS THIS WANDERER?

The Babylonian Jews lived in Babylon because their world had been turned upside down. Things they had previously considered impossible actually happened to them. They lost their homes in Israel and were forced into exile in Babylon. The Temple of God and the city where he had placed his name were destroyed by fire and left in rubble. How could God allow the enemy to destroy his own city and Temple? Kings would never rule again. Priests were displaced. Who would sacrifice for the people? Or pray for them? Could they still be the people of God while living in another nation? This exile to Babylon revealed the need for the people to have their own experience with God outside of the Temple.

Historians tell of a town whose name is roughly translated as "Judahtown," the name of the area in Babylon where the exiled people of Judah gathered and settled. We see similar situations in big cities where immigrants from other countries settle into their own neighborhoods, which then take on the character of their ancestral cultures. We can recognize this now in neighborhoods dubbed "Chinatown" or "Little Italy". Judahtown would have been much the same—a section of the town where the Jews had congregated and settled.

The Jews were not considered slaves while in Babylon. They more or less settled comfortably into Babylonian life. They even integrated with Babylonian culture, their own customs intertwining with those of Babylon. They owned houses, had gardens and fruit trees, and grew their families within the city's walls (see Jeremiah 29:5–7). Jews could become anything from agriculturalists to royal merchants to entrepreneurs who farmed, traded gold, or rented property. It wasn't uncommon for them to take out loans. Although a few were royal courtiers, most were farmers, poor and working hard to survive. Life there was surprisingly similar to life as we know it today.

Despite their status in Babylon, all Jews despised Babylonians for destroying their Temple and burning their houses when Jerusalem was taken. For hundreds of years thereafter, the word "Babylon" was synonymous with evil. Even so, most chose to stay in Babylon after they were given permission to leave and go home. For every Jew who walked back home, two stayed in Babylon. By then they had lived in Babylon for some seventy years. It would seem many did not want to leave their homes, their friends, or the lives they had built there.

Those who stayed had learned to live with their conquerors so comfortably that they didn't want to leave. And they stayed for thousands of years. In 1948 when the state of Israel was founded, Jews were still living in the area that was once ancient Babylon. It was too hard to go back. Maybe they forgot about Jerusalem, or perhaps they loved the stability of Babylon.

For the family in our story, it was a hunger to be in the city of God that led them to leave the comfort of the land in which they were raised. It was a chance to see the realization of their grandparent's dreams and the fulfillment of a promise their people had been given.

These Wanderers were to journey 1,678 miles from Babylon to Jerusalem. Not something you do on a random afternoon or without extensive thought and preparation. Imagine the planning, the supplies, the debating conversations. In comparison, the Oregon Trail was 2,170 miles, though the travel time would've been about the same since the nineteenth-century travelers had the advantage of covered wagons.

It is difficult to grasp how much mental and physical energy was required to walk with a family across a wilderness. The only similar experience I have would be a long car ride with our children, but still, that hardly holds a candle to wandering for months. Every Christmas, I would drive my wife and four kids to my parents' house, three-and-a-half hours away. We loved being with family, but no one was happy about getting in that minivan with five other people, and usually a dog, then driving forever on the interstate. We considered it a difficult trek, but by comparison it was infinitely easier. The children complained, but they sat comfortably the whole time. I can only imagine walking for four-to-five months. The daily frustrations, the challenges, and the demand to always push forward. It was difficult, dangerous, and exhausting.

The Wanderer in Psalm 107 was trying to make it back home to Jerusalem with his family, walking toward the Promised Land, but somehow getting lost along the way. They were looking for their city. A city represents security, stability, other people to connect with, a life to live, and something worth living for. According to the KJV, these people wandered in a solitary way, which indicates that they were on a lonely path, disconnected from others. They were misplaced and friendless.

These wandering travelers had grown up never knowing Jerusalem the way their ancestors had. They loved God and carried a hunger for him in their hearts, but they had only heard stories of what it was like to live there. Without ever experiencing it for themselves, each one had the importance of Jerusalem instilled in them from birth.

They weren't wandering because they didn't know God or because they desired the things of the world. No, they were on a path *away* from Babylon and heading *toward* their Promised Land. That's what made their wandering even more frustrating. They were doing what they were *supposed* to be doing.

But this is real life. Good people get off track. Christians sometimes lose their path. With tears in their eyes, they confess they love God but don't know where they are. Just like The Wanderer in our story, Christians can wander by accident, through no fault of their own, moving through life without clear direction. It just *happens*.

Wandering is a horrible time in anyone's life. The Wanderer no longer has a spot on the map to aim for, no turn-by-turn directions to follow; they've lost sight of their destination. Over time they become aimless. Walking and constantly on the move, they are unsettled in any location.

Wandering can look like walking. At first glance it may be hard to tell the difference between the two, but it's simple: Walking becomes wandering when the objective is lost. Without a known destination, one is wandering, continually moving without aim.

People who are spiritually wandering appear to be walking like other Christians, but in truth they have lost their way and desperately need a Guide to direct them.

Attend to me, and hear me;
I am restless in my complaint,
and moan noisily.

Psalm 55:2

Where are you going,
and where do you come from?

Judges 19:17b

TRAVELING OR DRIFTING?

A family member of mine recently found herself in a place without direction, not knowing what she was supposed to do with her future. From a young age, she had always been fascinated with American Sign Language (ASL) and felt that it was a calling from God on her life. When he led her to go to college for ASL, she followed.

She quit her job, started ASL classes, and was able to use what she was learning almost immediately when a young deaf boy started attending her church. But then her health started failing during her second year, and everything suddenly seemed to be falling apart. She couldn't keep up with her coursework or the part time jobs she had cobbled together to cover the cost of classes. Eventually, she felt she had no choice but to withdraw from school. When the deaf boy stopped coming to church shortly after, she assumed that God had her in ASL for only a season, maybe only for that one person, and that it was time to move on.

She was able to improve her health, switch to an

online degree, and graduate. She got a good job, started saving up her money, and bought a house. But she felt aimless. The feeling of fulfilled purpose was gone and she wasn't sure why.

One night she dreamed she was at a church conference in a convention hall. In the dream she had isolated herself and was working on a laptop away from the crowd when a man walked up to her and started talking to her in ASL. He wanted her to interpret the conference service. In a panic, she communicated that she couldn't do it. She was rusty. She didn't know enough. She wasn't practiced. The man in the dream was visibly disappointed, and as he walked away, she knew she had made a mistake. Her stomach began to hurt from the realization, and she woke up physically sick.

She prayed and asked God what she was supposed to do. She even asked for another dream with more details, and went to bed that night expecting it, but nothing happened for the next several nights.

Then on Saturday morning, she went hiking with a friend. They made sure to get to the state park very early, before it got too crowded, and they enjoyed having the entire area to themselves. So it was significant when, about an hour later, they came near two people. As they approached the couple, she recognized that the fuzzy white shape on one of their hoodies was a stylized ASL symbol for "I love you."

She called out to them, "I like your hoodie!"

They were looking right at her, but neither one

responded.

Then it hit her.

"I like your hoodie," she signed to the girl.

The girl's face lit up. *"You know sign?"*

The man then signed to her, *"We're lost."*

My family member was able to show them on the map where they were and how to get where they wanted to go.

It wasn't until she got back home that she realized how impossible that meeting was. There are relatively few deaf people in her state, and the majority of them live where the deaf school is. It's a small community and she had never met anyone deaf outside of that school or a dedicated deaf ministry. So the odds of her running into someone on an early Saturday morning, in a ravine, miles into a state park were unbelievably low.

She had asked God for direction, and he had sent two deaf people to find her and say, "We're lost." She was literally in The Wilderness when she met them—wandering in her own way, trying to find the path God wanted her to be on, searching for his will in her life.

For months she had felt lost and confused, and in that moment the unbelievable, excited feeling was like a return of purpose. Like coming back home.

———

Someone is likely standing in The Wanderer's shoes if they feel disconnected, stuck in their walk with God, out of sync with other believers, or without a clear guiding purpose or vision of what God is doing in and through their life. It's a restless, unsettled, searching-but-never-finding feeling. It's likely not anything inherently evil. It's hard to point to any one thing as *the mistake* responsible for someone's being off track.

Imagine them wandering through The Wilderness: restless, unsettled, stuck, unconnected, searching, and looking for answers they can never seem to find. They may not have realized it at first. Usually we don't. Every day is purposeful when one is headed somewhere in life. But when we lose our direction, we lose our purpose as well.

The Wanderer could not have avoided his Distress. He was a traveler heading back home who'd lost his way. He hadn't done anything wicked. God doesn't say that The Wanderer is the cause of his own troubles or that he needs to repent. Without realizing it, he just lost the right road and eventually found himself wandering—ever walking, never arriving.

How does this happen to us? When does life change from walking to wandering? We love the Lord, but somewhere on the journey, we somehow got off course. At some point along the path, purposeful walking turned to confused wandering

I know this story personally. I have been The Wanderer.

One month I was involved, working for God, serving in his kingdom, connecting to people, and living with a purpose. The next month I wasn't. Sometimes seasons change in our lives, and things shift. We don't always have control over those moments.

Most people describe this feeling as going through a dry season. It is painful to wander, especially when thinking of all the sacrifices one has made for God's kingdom. It hurts. There's a unique pain found in wandering—precisely because it happens while going in the right direction! That, to me, is the craziest part of this story.

I wasn't trying to do my own thing. I was trying to be pleasing to God. But then I walked through this difficult Wilderness without knowing what to do or how to change it. My only viable option was to seek God, pray with all my heart, and not give up.

One day something changed. Purpose and direction came back into my life. The Lord drew me into connections with those who needed me at that stage of my life. I knew it was the Lord because the circumstances had been beyond my ability to change. Only God was able to help me. And I could only trust and hold onto him during this time.

Throughout the Bible, we find examples of men we would consider mighty but who spent time wandering. Moses spent the better part of forty years on the backside of the wilderness, tending sheep. The only way to hear John the Baptist preach was to go out to the wilderness of Judea. David lived in Philistine territory for over a year while running from Saul. It would seem that the Lord is undaunted by The Wilderness times in our lives.

Spiritually, Wandering is not a place or a season anyone would choose to be part of. The Wilderness is something most of us avoid. It is a lonely place; there are no friends in The Wilderness. Spiritual Wanderers are not hungry for food or thirsty for water. They're hungry for a life that matters and thirsty for a place to belong.

The Wanderer can perhaps try harder or have a better attitude, but without clear direction, it won't matter. There is no one who can help him. No insight is available to him, no guide showing him what to do next. And there is simply no way to get out of the daily Wandering without divine intervention. The Wanderer desperately needs a Guide to show him the right path.

How can a person tell if they are Wandering endlessly in The Wilderness? Do they identify with The Wanderer? Did they start their walk with Jesus full of excitement and confidence, heading the right direction and living life on purpose, connected to other like-minded Christians? Somewhere along the journey did they lose the clarity and confidence they once had? Maybe something bad—or good—happened, or life got in the way. Once confident, they now feel like a raft caught in the eddies of the stream, going around and around, circling the same familiar rocks but never really going anywhere.

The psalmist said that God led The Wanderer by the right way, directing them to a city where they could live and settle down with stability and security (see

Psalm 107:7, 9). He satisfied the deep thirst of their souls and filled them with good things. God took them from loneliness to belonging.

O God! Have mercy on The Wanderer. Lead them out of this morass of life on to solid ground, and with a clear path.

— *Warning* —

Frustration is often part of The Wanderer's story because they are seeking God, trying to find the way out of their Wilderness, and attempting to continue their journey as a believer even though they don't know where they are or what they should do.

There is a danger that the Wanderer's frustration can turn against other people or even against God. Be careful not to become bitter against others who don't seem to understand our situation, and be careful not to get angry with God for allowing us to go through this difficult time. That mistake can cause us to become a wandering Rebel. The only thing we can do is to trust God. Call out to him and trust that he is working even when we can't prove it by our human senses.

Hear the Testimony of The Wanderer

You number my wanderings; put my tears into Your bottle; are they not in Your book? When I cry out to You, then my enemies will turn back; this I know, because God is for me. In God (I will praise His word), in the LORD (I will praise His word), in God I have put my trust; I will not be afraid. What can man do to me?

—Psalm 56:8–11, NKJV

They that go down to the sea in ships, that do business in great waters; these see the works of the LORD, and his wonders in the deep. For he commandeth, and raiseth the stormy wind, which lifteth up the waves thereof. They mount up to the heaven, they go down again to the depths: their soul is melted because of trouble. They reel to and fro, and stagger like a drunken man, and are at their wits' end. Then they cry unto the LORD in their trouble, and he bringeth them out of their distresses. He maketh the storm a calm, so that the waves thereof are still. Then are they glad because they be quiet; so he bringeth them unto their desired haven. Oh that men would praise the LORD for his goodness, and for his wonderful works to the children of men! Let them exalt him also in the congregation of the people, and praise him in the assembly of the elders.

Psalm 107:23–32

THE SAILOR

*Out of the depths have
I cried unto thee, O LORD.*

Psalm 103:1

ANOTHER DAY AT WORK

THE SAILOR

I hurried out the door, along the walk, and down the steps to the bustling dock. There wasn't even time to hug my wife. Experience taught that the ship wouldn't wait and I didn't want to face her with some lame excuse about why I'd overslept. We might be out for a week or two before I'd see home again.

If I had known what lay ahead, I would have taken the time to run back into the house. I would've stopped walking, turned around, and gone back up those steps to hug her tightly, lame excuse for oversleeping and all.

The dock was busy in the pre-dawn moonlight. The jostling of men moving supplies blended with the groaning of timber as they strained at the ropes to pull their cargo up the rough gangplanks. These familiar sounds, punctuated by the thud of goods being loaded into the hold, confirmed that I had arrived at work.

I'm a sailor on a merchant ship, tasked with moving goods from one port to another. Sometimes our cargo is metal, sometimes wood, and occasionally food.

My job is manning an oar, but other work starts while we're still in port: unfolding the stiff canvas sails, pulling up the stone anchors, and securing the cargo.

This is my life and the only work I know. I suppose it's not a surprising line of work for a son in the tribe of Zebulon. Our people are seafaring; we live on the seashore. The symbol for our tribe is a ship. Sailing is in our blood.

A few more ships would join us soon after clearing port, and the entire fleet would sail across the Mediterranean.

The job is demanding. And though our bodies are strong with muscles built from years of rowing, the scars that decorate those muscles bear witness to the pain of previous journeys and remind even the roughest of men there's no guarantee we'll all make it home.

I don't enjoy being gone from my family for weeks at a time, but what can I do? This is my life. All of my friends struggle with the same difficulties. Our wives take care of the kids and the house until we return home. If I made it back, I would be thankful not to have to leave again, at least for a few days.

Out of habit I checked the moon and the constellations above me. It was unnecessary because just like every other sailor, I had already checked the sky yesterday and then again early this morning. Nothing troubling showed on the horizon. We all knew how vital it was to be aware of the weather. Any storm activity, even distant from us, was worth paying attention to—

an occupational necessity. No bag of coins was worth fighting through a deadly storm.

As a small boy, I remember hearing Father talk about the red sky at night, reassuring Mother that it would be a good day of sailing on the deep. A red sky in the morning was a sign to stay home. But the moon looked clear, no halo around it last night or this morning. A little rain wouldn't stop us, but I was glad we wouldn't face contrary winds.

Finally, everything was settled, stowed, tied down, and ready for our voyage. I found my spot port side, four rows back from the front, and got into position. Time to work. The grumbling and chatter stopped as we moved away from the dock.

Yahweh, keep your hand upon us through this journey.

Rows of hands pulled on oars, easily falling into the rhythm of the ship. The first line of a galley song drifted through the air and all the men joined in. We would have made a terrible choir, but the pacing of the words helped move the ship along as we chanted and pulled our oars in unison.

My shoulders started hurting as we glided out of the bay. It was an old injury, and I knew from experience that the pain would eventually ease. But still, I hoped we wouldn't be fighting through many strong winds on this voyage.

For all my complaints about how tough the job is, there are wonderful benefits. No one on land would ever understand the miracles we see in the great water.

The color of the sea as it changes from early daylight to afternoon is magnificent. Today the morning sun peeked over the horizon, and the water was a crystal-clear blue. But I knew it could change to a shade that challenged the depths of the deepest green, appearing black as the weather turned. The struggles of death and life could happen just off the tip of my oar. Magnificent beasts chased their prey, and we'd yell out whenever we caught sight of teeth catching a fin, watching in fascination as the blood bubbled up to the surface. I've survived everything from strong winds and killer waves to the deathly quiet of windless days when the sails hang flat and there's only the heaving of shoulder and oar to push us through the waters.

We would be on the water for less than a week—if the fair winds held—before reaching port. Then a day or two rejuvenating in port before heading back, which would take roughly the same amount of time. Thinking of the day or two we'd enjoy on land helped keep me pushing. We were sailing with a full crew, which meant us oarsmen would be free to explore the port on our own while the ship was being unloaded and reloaded and money changed hands. I'd indulge in moments of peace and relaxation. And there was a shop I would stop at to buy a little something for my girl.

This trip was looking favorable. No warnings. No worries. A quiet night after a long morning.

*He reached down from on high and took
hold of me; he drew me out of deep waters.
He rescued me from my powerful enemy,
from my foes, who were too strong for me.*

Psalm 18:16–17 (NIV)

THE STORM

THE SAILOR

When everything is working and everyone is pulling together, the boat slips quickly through the waters. We have to be one with the sea. The water is too big and too powerful to wrestle. One cannot fight her and win; a sailor learns early on to work with whatever she gives.

The routine keeps things going, each day slipping into the next. Row. Rest. Row. Rest. Help your fellow workers when you can and hope for fair weather. Sometimes when my muscles ache, I pray for a strong wind at our back to push us through the water. When we get a leeward wind, we barely even need to row.

I was sandwiched between two other oarsmen. Between that and the tackle to my right, I could just catch glimpses of the port side between the rhythmic dip and splash of the other oars. A school of fish passed and dove but didn't resurface. A flock of gulls flew overhead, aiming straight toward the shore.

Thinking back, something about the water gave me a vague sense of unease, as though my gut knew something my mind hadn't yet figured out. The sea had been quiet, but now it seemed too quiet. Maybe it was the way the sweat turned cold on my skin. It felt wrong, like nature was telling me something my brain hadn't picked up on.

A shout came from the bow, startling me out of my stupor. The wind shifted. All oars were lifted out of the water, and we held them there for a moment as we studied the clouds.

There was going to be trouble. We could see it in the menace of the billowing clouds. A wave slammed the bow and thrust it into the air, and for a moment I lost my grip on my oar. Thankfully, it couldn't go overboard while in the oarlock. I secured it and hurried to help with the sail. Sudden winds were pounding on our mainsail, spinning us in the water. We had to get it down fast.

Rain pelted my face as we got the sail down, roughly folded it, and forced it into place between the rowers. Anything not tied down was soon lost to the sea. We tried to grab, hold, tie down, or wrap everything around us either in a net or with a rope, but the ship began pitching up and down like a bucking donkey. Our shouts were swallowed up in the screaming wind, and we could only pass directions by yelling man to man.

Our first instinct was to row our way out of this storm. I tried to get back to my seat, staggering like a drunk, reaching for and missing the mast. Supplies were rolling around the deck of the ship. The bow shot up in the air and held there for a few seconds before plunging into a deep trough.

I thought of things I could try to do, but they all seemed futile. The shipmaster screamed for rowers to get to their posts. If we pushed hard enough with our oars, maybe we could keep the ship from capsizing or breaking apart. Maybe we could row out of the storm as it blew past. I held on to sea-soaked rigging, still trying to get back to my spot. When I finally sat and grabbed my oar, I noticed several of the crew were missing.

Had they fallen overboard? I couldn't see anyone in the water. And in this screaming wind no one could have heard their cries for help. Those of us who could drop our oars back into the sea tried in vain to redirect the ship, aiming for the sweet spot on each breaking wave. Even if we had every hand working together, I don't know if we could have controlled the ship. But we surely couldn't control it now.

This could be the end.

The other boats in the fleet were in the same life-and-death melee with no one to help, no one to send. We were in the middle of the beast, far from land and farther from any port. I might never see my precious wife again. My family would only be able to guess how it ended for me.

We were too far from land to swim. Nobody knew where we were, and *we* didn't know where we were. The skies were black, and the winds had long pushed us hard off course. There would be places, islands, rocky spots we did *not* want the vessel to hit. In this full-force gale, we could be driven into a rock and be smashed to pieces.

There was no glimpse of light or sign that we could get out by rowing in any given direction. I hate to admit it, but I gave up. No place to hide. No muscles strong enough to pull us out of this disaster. All the riches in the world couldn't get us out.

Let not the floodwater overflow me,
nor let the deep swallow me up;
and let not the pit shut its mouth on me.

Psalm 69:15

A HOPELESS END

THE SAILOR

This storm didn't make sense. We had been so careful to check the weather, to be prepared, to avoid a storm. If we had only known, the ship would have waited in port for a few days. Nothing was worth this. I wished I really would've overslept that morning. Why had I worked so hard to get on this ship?

Was a little money worth my life? The pilot could have guided us into one of several ports we had passed by. At one point, someone had mentioned how it would be nice to stop there for a night. The shipmaster overheard it, and with a withering look, spat out, "No. We're pushing through." Of course he did. We were being paid to bring this merchandise to port, and they would pay us better for arriving quickly. But now there would be no payment. Any goods still on board would soon sink to the bottom along with the ship itself.

I could have stayed home. Why hadn't I stayed home? I would be safe, dry, and missing the storm. I wanted to be home with my wife. I wanted my family. Mostly, I wanted quiet. Away from the booming clamor of the storm. The chaos of things blowing around. The lines snapping in the wind with enough power to put out someone's eye. The pounding rain. The screaming wind. The unceasing waves slapping against the ship. I wanted it all to stop. I wanted peace. One moment the ship was pointed toward the sky; then we were plummeting into a trough. Down to hell. Where my body would be eventually buried.

This storm was not my fault, but it didn't matter. I was in it, and I would drown all the same. I did nothing wrong, but the waves didn't care.

Hope seemed lost. I finally gave up trying to row. Everyone else already had. My heartbeat was in my throat as I sat there, dazed, watching the destruction of the ship. I could only hope to hang on until the end. *So this is what it feels like to take my last breaths.* Saltwater in my mouth. The wind deafening my ears. Fear crushing my heart. Nothing any of us could do would get us out of this storm. No one would bury me in the family grave or perform last rites over my body. I would sink into these dark waters forever, food for the creatures of the deep.

Oh, for a Captain to lead me out of this madness and into a peaceful harbor.

The Sailor's Prayer

O Captain of my salvation, reach down from heaven and take hold of me. Pull me out of these deep waters. Rescue me from my powerful enemy, from drowning in this storm. I'm not strong enough to survive this without your help, O Lord. This is an emergency call for help. God, only you can save me.

—Paraphrase of Psalm 18:16–17

Your riches, wares, and merchandise,
Your mariners and pilots,
Your caulkers and merchandisers,
All your men of war who are in you,
and the entire company which is in
your midst, will fall into the midst
of the seas on the day of your ruin.

Ezekiel 27:27 (NKJV)

JUST WORKING

If we had seen The Sailor on the morning of the great storm, we wouldn't have noticed anything unusual. The Sailor didn't have clue that this day would be anything other than normal. He worked on the boat, tied a line, and repaired a sail. Just doing his job. Sailors paid careful attention to the weather, especially the possibility of storms. If there had been any warning about a storm like that, he would have stayed safe on dry land. The storm blew up in a moment. It wasn't his fault, and there was no way to avoid it.

As his world filled with turmoil, The Sailor's courage melted away. Can you see him stumbling and staggering like a drunken man, flailing like a newborn unable to stand up? Can you picture him trying to hold on to something—anything—as the ship bucks and the wind screams and anything not tied down gets blown overboard? Can you see the shock on his face as the ship pitches downward into another trough? He isn't thinking about how he got into this problem. His only thought is survival.

There is absolutely nothing he could have done to stop this storm. No possible way to get away from it or find a safe place to hide. Nobody could have helped him out in the deep waters. The Sailor needed a Captain to lead him to a safe harbor.

The book of Ecclesiastes says, "Time and chance happen to them all" (9:11c, NIV). And Paul writes, "such as is common to man" (1 Corinthians 10:13).

Jesus told a story about two kinds of people who listen to his words and built houses. Both were attacked by the same powerful storm. Both were beaten by driving rains, sweeping floods, and mighty winds. Only one remained standing—the one built on a solid foundation. No one escapes The Storms Jesus spoke about. It's part of living. We cannot choose to avoid The Storm. We can, however, choose to build our lives on his Word so that we'll be standing when The Storm is over.

Storms of death sweep in unexpectedly and take loved ones from us. Financial Storms turn our comfortable lives upside down. Physical Storms can arrive in a moment, leaving us with lasting pain and debilitation. Relational Storms can explode, eroding and destroying our trust.

A Storm is a trial, a powerful event that threatens to destroy our lives and swallow us up in grief (1 Peter 1:6). These Storms bring winds that tear things apart and waves that beat and crush our lives. Search the Bible and you'll find plenty of people trying to survive

Storms. From Job and Jonah to David, the disciples, and even Jesus himself.

The Storm is immense, and the impact is evident, but the lead-up to The Storm is not always so obvious. Everyone can see The Storm when it hits, but it gathers outside our recognition. One can usually tell when someone in their community is caught in a Storm. They're the ones who clearly need emergency prayer.

While sitting in calm weather with a shining sun, it's easy to decide what we'll do during a Storm. Unfortunately, we can't necessarily plan for it, and we don't always know how we will react until one shows up. But if we make a point of always clinging to God, that's where we'll be when it hits.

Deadly Storms can show up in the middle of a normal day—when we're at work or taking care of our family, when traveling or relaxing. Surprise is part of the impact of The Storm. You don't see it coming. Life is good. Then The Storm hits.

One such Storm showed up for us on a weekend and blew our world apart.

My wife noticed something that felt different when she got dressed. She wanted to get it checked out, just to be extra careful. The doctor confirmed that there was a lump, and after a series of exams and testing we were told it was cancer.

Up to that point in our lives, we knew just a couple of things about cancer. One, it was something *other* people experienced, and we prayed for them.

Second, we had decided early in our marriage that if either of us got cancer, we would just let it run its course. We had reasoned that people who went through all the chemo and radiation seemed to be in worse health and in a lot more pain, and they didn't seem to live much longer anyway. In fact, their health seemed to fail even more rapidly once the treatment started.

But everything is different when *you* are in The Storm.

Jenn told me that she felt that she had to fight this cancer for our boys, who were still at home, and for our daughter, who was now raising her own baby girl.

She would fight to stay alive for our family.

What a change in our lives. We were tossed onto a roller coaster of doctors, hospitals, insurance companies, prayer, worry, and whatever faith we could muster. We walked the line between trusting in a sovereign God and staring death in the face. And we prayed. We prayed and fasted and had others pray. Our family prayed. Our friends prayed. People we'd never met prayed. We asked for the cancer to be healed. We knew God *could* deliver her supernaturally, we knew he could change the situation at any time, but he didn't.

The Lord did not *spare* us from that Storm, but he did take us *through* it. We don't know why he allowed it, but he showed himself as our protector every step of the way through it.

Even though the miracle we wanted did not come, God still provided miraculously all along the way, and many situations proved he was there with us.

Jenn has been cancer free for many years now. We still cannot answer the question of why God allowed this to happen, but we held on to our faith that God was with us *through* it.

It's no use to be angry at The Storm. Sure, The Sailor could have stayed home that day, or perhaps the ship could've taken an alternate route. Everyone would do something differently if they could know the future. Screaming at The Storm doesn't help. The waves and wind are unaffected and uninterested by anyone's anger and hurt. The best thing The Sailor could do was latch on to something solid and try to outlast The Storm. But even that effort would have been useless without a rescuer, a Captain to lead him to safe harbor.

A furious squall came up, and the waves broke over the boat, so that it was nearly swamped. Jesus was in the stern, sleeping on a cushion. The disciples woke him and said to him, "Teacher, don't you care if we drown?"

Mark 4:37–38 (NIV)

SURVIVING THE STORM

It is often the case that things lost in The Storm are never recovered. In the Acts 27 storm the sailors threw things overboard to lighten the ship and hopefully survive. In the end, they lost everything on board, including the ship, but their lives were saved. The Storms we go through will most often take things from us. Yes, Jesus can do anything, but often he allows Storms to blow through our lives. And they are painful.

Look what God did in answer to The Sailor's cry for help: He calmed The Storm so that the waves were still.

> Then they cry unto the LORD in their trouble,
> And he bringeth them out of their distresses.
> He maketh the storm a calm,
> So that the waves thereof are still.
> Then are they glad because they be quiet;
> So he bringeth them unto their desired haven.
> (Psalm 107:28–30)

This word from God in Psalm 107 applies to all who are staggering, stumbling, or shaken from a monstrous, life-rattling Storm.

Make no mistake, God's will and work in The Storm is not the same for every situation. Sometimes he rebukes The Storm, but just as often he brings the calm to his child. Sometimes he allows the winds to continue to blow. In Acts 16 Paul testified that God delivered him and Silas from prison. But in Acts 23 God allowed Paul to stay in prison for more than two years. God was with him in both the prison break *and* the prison stay.

As Christians, how do we know if we're in a Storm? When we're fighting in a Storm, we are trying to survive. Life was good, or at least normal, before The Storm—before that call, before those test results, before the job was lost. Now there is only the sense of not being able to fix it and not knowing what to do. Our faith has been rocked, and our world is topsy-turvy. Once firmly held beliefs about God and life become suddenly flimsy and untethered. Maybe even our core belief in God has been shaken. We may be hanging on for dear life in the trial of our lives and needing immediate help.

It's fruitless to try and examine what could have been done to avoid it. The Storm comes through no fault of our own. The only thing we can do is hold on tight to the Lord and refuse to let go. We may analyze why The Storm is happening, but we cannot control the monstrous waves or quiet the shrieking winds. Any ability or way out of this trial has been lost, swallowed up, or whipped away in the wind.

There wasn't a single thing The Sailor could have done to prevent this Storm. He had to turn to the only one with the power over the wind and waves. He could not escape because there was no safe place to hide from The Storm, and no effort on his part would have made a difference. A better attitude cannot stop a ship from spinning out of control. Having more determination to paddle or to solve the question of The Storm will not make a difference when the waves are higher than the mast. When someone is in a Storm like this, their only option is to cry out to God. The Sailor desperately needed a Captain who could guide him through The Storm.

The psalmist says God rescued The Sailor, and he was glad because of the calm and quiet. Finally, God brought him to the harbor he longed for.

*But now I urge you to keep up your
courage, because not one of you will
be lost; only the ship will be destroyed.
Last night an angel of the God to whom
I belong and whom I serve stood beside
me and said, "Do not be afraid."*

Acts 27:22–24a (NIV)

RESCUE

The Sailor couldn't say exactly when The Storm started, just as The Wanderer didn't know at what point he stopped walking in the right direction. Both were in deep Distress, a trouble that they did not cause. And neither could get themselves out of their mess through their own strength or ingenuity.

The Wilderness of The Wanderer is a slow death by hunger and thirst. But The Storm is a 911 call, a sudden attack or loss. The internal is usually under attack in The Wilderness. It drains our faith, our trust in God, our peace. The external is usually under attack in The Storm. The Storm comes for family, for finances, for the physical body.

The Wanderer is out with his family, attempting to find his way to a city. The Sailor leaves his family at home and goes to work with a crew. The Wanderer carries the marks of his environment, his face and clothing grimy with the sand and dirt from carrying his tent and supplies. The Sailor also has distinctive marks of calluses on his hands and scars on his arms from years of trimming sails, casting nets, and pulling in anchors.

Both need help. If either of them decides to give up on God, they will be forever lost. There is no salvation available to The Wanderer in The Wilderness around him. He's tried everything he can think of to solve this problem on his own. The Sailor has also attempted to do everything he can to get out from under this dark cloud and away from The Storm. If either one could save themselves, they would have already done so.

Both The Wanderer and The Sailor are going through situations they can't explain. Both are innocent of the trials they are experiencing. Their locations are physically far apart, but they both require help in their Distress. They need someone bigger than them, someone who has the answers and the power to lead them out.

Human hope can't last forever, especially in the face of an immediate crisis. The Sailor may have had hope The Storm would break. He may have hoped that he could have maneuvered the ship out of the worst of The Storm with some help from his fellow oarsmen. But as the waves continued to beat on the ship, he would've begun to lose hope of ever seeing his family again. The Sailor needed a hope higher than himself. He needed something better than luck or a good break. He turned his cries for help toward heaven, the only hope available to him.

I can say to The Sailor with certainty that God loves us. He sees us about to capsize, close to drowning in deep waters that no one could survive. As we cry to

God with all our heart, he will reach down and pull us out of those deep waters.

Hebrews 13:5 reminds us of Jesus' promise that "I will never leave you nor forsake you." God is with us. We can hold this thought in our minds while The Storm winds beat against our lives. In the worst of our troubles, in the darkest days, in endless nights, God has never left us. And he never will.

— *Warning* —

Fear is present in every powerful Storm. There's no pretending to be calm in the face of a life-threatening situation. Be aware that you still have a *choice*, even in the worst of situations. If you allow fear to have its way, it will lead you away from God. The best course of action for any Sailor in a Storm is to cry out to God, to run to the only One who can rescue you.

Hear the Testimony of The Sailor

O LORD God of hosts, who is mighty like You, O LORD? Your faithfulness also surrounds You. You rule the raging of the sea; when its waves rise, You still them.

—Psalm 89:8–9, NKJV

Such as sit in darkness and in the shadow of death, being bound in affliction and iron; because they rebelled against the words of God, and contemned the counsel of the Most High: therefore he brought down their heart with labour; they fell down, and there was none to help. Then they cried unto the LORD in their trouble, and he saved them out of their distresses. He brought them out of darkness and the shadow of death, and brake their bands in sunder. Oh that men would praise the LORD for his goodness, and for his wonderful works to the children of men! For he hath broken the gates of brass, and cut the bars of iron in sunder.

Psalm 107:10–16

THE REBEL

I called on Your name, O LORD, from
the lowest pit. You have heard my voice:
"Do not hide Your ear from my
sighing, from my cry for help."

Lamentations 3:55–56 (NKJV)

CHASING FUN

THE REBEL

I suppose I have a thick head. Don't like to admit this, but I guess I don't listen very well to anybody. Pain has a way of getting my attention, though, so now I'll do whatever it takes. Just get me out of this horrible place!

This wasn't always my story. I had better days, free to do what I wanted. Friends to see. Things to do. Places to go. A special someone. I loved her, but I lost her along with everything else. My greatest punishment is not the chains that rub my ankles raw or the hard labor of working in the fields like a beast. No, it's thinking of the ones I've hurt. The ones who loved me and tried to save me from this bitter end.

I can barely survive on the meager slop I eat. The pain in my body from the innumerable beatings and exhaustion-induced falls is beyond description. Yet the gnawing pain in my mind is greater than any other. I am punished endlessly day and night by how easily I could have avoided this place.

When I'm allowed to go back to my cell, my

mind is free to remember the people I loved, the ones who are now cut off from me. I remember being warned about this Prison. I remember laughing about it right in their faces. I hear my mother's prayers for me and I am tormented.

My former life was good. I was free and easy. My parents were hardworking. I was surrounded by solid people with ordinary routines and predictable days with ordinary friends. I was raised to learn the family business and to one day take over and carry on my father's good name. But I despised being predictable. I didn't want to be ordinary. I didn't want to be stuck in that little corner of the world where I had been born.

Earlier in my youth something switched in my mind. Maybe it was a cousin of mine who started me thinking this way, or maybe he just egged me on to where I was already headed. But I decided I was finished listening to anyone who told me how to live because I could see how my life would likely end up. I would work every day like a dog, making the same pitiful money on which my parents barely survived, and I'd marry some homely girl who lived nearby.

Not for me. I was determined to see the world, have fun, and find an exciting life even if I had to fight for it. And fight I did. I fought everyone around me. I fought against my parents, my uncles, the local priest, and anyone else who tried to make me change.

I used to sneak away with my cousin, and we would walk to the big city in search of amusement. It was exciting. There were pretty girls and some eye-opening places to be around, especially for a country bum like me. Sure, I found myself in a few fights, and there were some scary people in some dark places, but that was part of the fun. The high risk of trouble made the thrill of being there so much greater. Who wants boring days when you can have wild nights? It might not have been the wise thing to do, but it was the fun thing to do. Besides, isn't it old people who are supposed to be wise? I figured there'd be enough time for me to have wisdom later. The arguments with my parents filled most of my days now anyway. Threats and warnings rained down on my head, but I didn't listen a bit. I was hunting for excitement, and most of the time I found it.

I'll never forget slipping back into the house early one morning before sunrise and hearing my mother pray for me. She was crying softly and calling my name out to God. Hearing that cut deep inside, and I never forgot the feeling. It was impossible to get to sleep that night. I couldn't shake her prayers. But in the morning, I set my mind and made my heart like a stone. Nothing was more important to me than living my life *my* way. No prayers were going to keep *me* tied up in this worthless village.

*And the LORD God of their fathers
sent warnings to them by His messengers,
rising up early and sending them, because
He had compassion on His people
and on His dwelling place.*

2 Chronicles 36:15 (NKJV)

WARNINGS

THE REBEL

As I grew older, I had more freedom to do what I wanted and live wherever a friend would take me in for the night. I still worked with Dad here and there, but not consistently, just long enough to make a little money that I would spend on fun someplace else. He wasn't happy with that or with me, and he told me so. I never hit my father, but some of our arguments were so heated that I wanted to.

I hated that I couldn't escape from villagers who knew me. Even far from home in some stupid little market or in the back of some dark tavern, somebody would recognize me. One time an old woman came up to me right there in the street. I guess my mom used to buy loaves of her special bread.

"Listen to me, young man. You are headed straight for trouble."

I laughed, of course.

"This is not funny."

It was like she didn't notice me mocking her. She just got more intense. "Hear me when I say that you are running away from Yahweh, child. One day you will regret what you are doing. Do you remember the Scripture passage I used to teach you? You must love the Lord your God with all your heart, all your soul, and all your strength. You aren't only turning your back on your parents; you're turning your back on God. Do you want to fight against God?"

That made me angry.

"Do you know how dumb that sounds? Nobody can fight God. How can you reach up to Heaven and punch him? And you can't run away from a God who's everywhere, right? I do remember *that* Scripture. But I am not going to follow it because I'll never regret having fun. So leave me alone."

She shook her head and walked away. I don't think she understood. I wasn't confused about God's Word. I knew what my parents had taught me. I could still quote the sayings of Moses. I wasn't confused, and I hadn't forgotten. I simply refused to listen.

A few months later while I was walking through a big market, a man making leather goods saw me browsing by his table and called out my name. I didn't remember him, but I guess he knew my father. Said he worked with him when I was a baby.

"I saw your mom and dad a couple of weeks ago on my way back from the festival. Your mother is worried about you." He turned away from the table to stack the straps and harnesses before going on. "I know what it's like to be angry with the world, son."

A good sneer usually shuts people up, but apparently not this guy.

He continued, "I tried to fight life. I argued with my family, and my life was a wreck. I figure that you may not hear one word of what I'm saying, but I still have to tell you. I've got to try. If you stay on this road long enough, you will run into pain. This way of living will only bring agony, trust me.

"God is reaching for you. This isn't an accident that you came by my booth today. Listen to me, young man. You can still turn your life around. You don't have to keep going this way. I wish someone would've cared enough to say these same things to me back then."

I raised my hand in mock appreciation. "Thanks, *friend*. I'll . . . keep that in mind."

I walked away laughing at his stupidity. I didn't even know him. Now *that* was funny. Why couldn't these people just let me be? I only wanted to see the world, have loads of fun, and do it all my own way. What was wrong with that?

My life slowly slipped into a pattern of making a little money, blowing it on whatever excited me, and doing it all over again. I stopped seeing my parents. I was old enough to live alone and do what I wanted. It was better to avoid them. Life wasn't pretty or simple. I couldn't always find the easy money like I had hoped would play out, and moving around made it difficult to get good work. I had a few scrapes, sometimes with the law, most times just with some idiot I ran into. But I was surviving, I was making it.

My entire life pivoted on that fateful day when consequences finally caught up with me.

It was too tempting a prize to pass up. Some of my friends told me about a risky way to make some serious money. I'm not a thief, but how often does an opportunity come along to steal treasure from a Babylonian prince? Imagine not having to work again for a *year*.

I planned it out perfectly.

And I almost got away with it.

I had made it out of the tent with the jewels in my pocket. I'd just slipped right in and right back out. I lifted the tent flap and started out, soaring because I'd pulled it off. I'd only taken a couple of steps when the sharp-eyed guard saw me. He wasn't supposed to be here! I knew because I'd gone over my escape route countless times. I'd tracked his schedule every day for a week, but I didn't plan for him to forget something and go back to his post. I tried to put on an innocent face and slip away, but he wasn't fooled. I was not supposed to be anywhere near that tent. Two little seconds, that's all I'd needed. That, or a sleepy guard on duty. But of course not. No luck for me.

He grabbed my arm, and the jewels clinked alarmingly in my pocket. The jig was up. My life was over.

I was frisked, bound, and tossed on the ground before the prince. I seriously thought my life was over.

The prince would kill me right there on the spot. This man did not hold to the law of Moses so he could have. Instead, he wanted me to pay for my crimes with the rest of my life and never be free to steal again.

Now I live here in the shadows, forgotten in a filthy prison, bound with iron chains and shackled under a life sentence. The prince had instructed the jailer to put me under heavy labor. I was to spend any remaining time in darkness. My body hurts every day. My heart is swallowed in misery, and my thoughts haunt me whenever I am pushed back into my cell. This is hell on earth, but it's a Prison I earned of my own rebellion.

No one else is at fault. I did it to myself.

Listen to the moaning of the prisoners.
Demonstrate your great power by
saving those condemned to die.

Psalm 79:11 (NLT)

PRISON

THE REBEL

When I was first imprisoned, I kept track of the days, but I don't recall when I stopped. At the beginning I only thought about when I could get out, like everybody else I suppose. I marked a little stone for each day that passed. I listened in on conversations, hoping against hope that I would discover a way to escape. Back in those days, I would daydream about breaking down the door or punching through the back wall—if I could only muster the strength of Samson.

Day by day, my hope slowly died. I don't know where it went, but hope no longer lives in this cell, and I no longer mark the days. The prison is dark, and no one cares about us. We are cut off from family and friends. I don't know if my parents are living or dead, and that hurts worse than another beating. Oh, to get out of here and go back home. To sit down at my old table with my parents and tell them how sorry I am. But what if they've passed? I'll never have a chance to make it right. Just thinking that is a cruel joke though because I can't leave. And even if I could, I could never make anything right.

Every morning the prisoners are taken out to the field, and our chains are attached to a plow or press. We push and pull and work like animals. Should anyone try to rest, the lash quickly finds their back and strikes pain through their whole body.

My body shows the scars and wounds of my life as a prisoner. No one can rescue me from this. I don't think my family or old friends even know where I am. There are no visits, no messages. No one checks on us or even pretends to care that we live or die.

There's only one way out of here: death. The executioner will call for me one day if I haven't already died from the pain. Either way, my life will end. What a waste. This is worse than being stupid. This wasn't me being clueless about the right way to live. No, I completely understood.

When I get back to my cell, and my leg chains are reattached, I sit against the dirty wall in the darkness and think about the Scriptures I learned as a child. Back then, everyone was excited about how quickly I could recite the words of the prophets or Moses. After a short time of hearing them, they would simply stick in my head, and it was simple to repeat them for the priest.

Mom thought I would become a top student or maybe even a religious leader one day. In another life, I would be a teacher of the Torah. I can see myself dressed in robes, talking to children who want to be me someday. Instead, I've destroyed my life. If anyone talks about me to children now, it's a cautionary tale.

I pull absent-mindedly at the collar around my neck. It hurts, and it restricts my movements. Look at me: chained to a rock, wasting away day by day. I shouldn't be here. This isn't what I was meant to do. No one could ever get out of these chains without a key. I know, I've tried many times. What little food I'm given is not enough to sustain me for the work I do every day. My arms have become smaller than they should be, and I have grown weak. A few days ago, I got back to my cell and fell to the floor, too weak to stand.

This is the end. My body cannot keep up. Will I last another month? Even another week?

Oh, how I long for a Deliverer. Someone who would come to set me free and lead me home.

The Rebel's Prayer

LORD, you are merciful, forgiving, and full of loving-kindness. I have rebelled against you. I refused to pay attention to your voice when you showed me how to live, through the words of the prophets. Now God, please deliver me. Hear my prayers and my petitions. I know it is my fault that this has happened. I'm not asking for your help because I am righteous, but because of your great mercy.

—Paraphrased from Daniel 9:9–10 and 17–18

*The Spirit of the LORD GOD is upon
Me, because the LORD has anointed
Me to preach good tidings to the poor;
He has sent Me to heal the brokenhearted,
to proclaim liberty to the captives,
and the opening of the prison
to those who are bound.*

Isaiah 61:1 (NKJV)

THOSE WHO ARE BOUND

Who is this Rebel, and how did he get into Prison? We don't know exactly what The Rebel did. The Bible doesn't tell us what sin built his iron cell, but the overall picture is clear: The Rebel heard the words of God and refused to listen. He rejected the light and inevitably ended up in darkness, sentenced to a life of hard labor behind bars.

The Rebel clearly heard and understood what God commanded yet turned away. There is no excuse of misunderstanding in this depiction. Stubborn and argumentative, The Rebel did only what *he* wanted to do. God sent him wise counsel. It was through other people, of course, because that's how God generally works. Someone gave him God-directed advice, and he kicked it away. Possibly he heard a testimony, a message of godly wisdom, or even a rebuke that seemed harsh at the time, but he mocked it. He laughed at the simple people who lived by all those rules and guidelines.

The psalm writer's description of The Rebel's confinement might be the actual treatment of captives by Assyrian and Babylonian soldiers of the time. The cells for prisoners were very dark, and the threat of execution always hung over them. Abuse and beatings were common. They were condemned to what was referred to as "the shadow of death." These captives were separated from friends and family, wearing only the rags of prisoners and working only for their captors to profit from their labor.

The Rebel is worn out from working as a slave, and no one can help him. He sits in darkness, a place of misery and death, out of sight of the rest of the world. The shadow of death is place nobody wants to visit. That's not a holiday spot on anyone's wish list. When someone was tossed in a Babylonian prison, it was an eventual death sentence. There was no advocate or attorney in those days to take on their case. A prisoner usually worked until they died, unless they were executed in the meantime.

This Prison was a place of weeping, of Distress, a place very close to the world of the dead. The Rebel traded his precious life and freedom for imprisonment. He remained bound in iron, a captive in a harsh cage.

The Rebel didn't immediately call out to God. Even while in Prison, for a long time he refused to call out to God. He was a Rebel after all. He knew what God had said. He knew the Scriptures. He understood what he should do—what his loved ones were asking. Yet he intentionally refused. His suffering in darkness didn't move him to pray. Being in Prison with iron chains wasn't enough to cause him to call on God.

It had to get even worse than that.

It's hard to comprehend having to get any lower in misery and agony, but The Rebel had to go even lower to reach the bottom. Finally, God allowed him to be under hard labor, with his pride broken under heaviness, where he fell to the ground. He stumbled and fell hard. Nobody could help him. He lay there on the filthy cold floor, tangled in his own chains like the animal he had become.

Then, and only then, did The Rebel cry out to the Lord in his trouble.

Release my soul from prison so
that I may give thanks to your name.
Righteous people will surround me
because you are good to me.

Psalm 142:7 (NOG)

SOUL PRISON

It would be easy for The Rebel to pinpoint the moment his life changed course for the worse. He need only look back to those times he rejected God's Word, laughing in the face of holy wisdom. The Rebel had plenty of time to sit and ruminate on the times he despised godly insights and warnings from loved ones and spiritual leaders. When did he last hear someone begging him to let go of his stubborn ways, turn his heart back, and humble himself before God?

All that was long ago, seemingly in a different life.

Now he sits in darkness, imprisoned by impenetrable bronze gates, bound in iron chains, hidden from the world, alone and far away from all who loved him. No one can see or visit him. He lives in a cage he created, made by his willful rebellion against God.

The Rebel needs a Deliverer to cut through the bars and chains and set him free. He cannot get free of this Prison by himself. If he could, it wouldn't be a Prison, and he wouldn't be a captive. These are not chains made of paper mâché. He's captured behind brass gates and iron bars. No human effort can deliver him from this dungeon. No one on Earth can truly help him.

This is a story I know personally. I have been a similar type of Rebel. I've never been incarcerated or struggled with a substance addiction, but I talked and acted like The Rebel.

I felt it was so unfair that my parents decided to move us away from the big churches to pastor a little country church in a podunk town surrounded by farmers. I latched onto the idea that every other teenager in the world was out there enjoying life while I sat here missing out. Anger and frustration swept into my life, and I began to push back on everything and everyone. I didn't run away or do drugs, but I rebelled in every other area.

I had a nasty attitude and a prideful, cocky, I-know-better-than-you mentality that made me difficult to be around. It was a particularly horrible time for my parents. I argued with anyone who spoke to me, and even with people who came to visit my mother, their pastor's wife. I told adults they were flat wrong, and I made my Christian school teacher cry and run out of the classroom. I told anyone who would listen that I would never preach the gospel or be a pastor like my dad. I declared I would rather be like Jonah.

My mom was always fasting and praying that God would "get ahold of me" because no one else could.

But that didn't get me to change.

When I was about seventeen years old, life was sweet. I got a job, a car, and a girlfriend. Then one summer afternoon God got my attention by allowing me to experience more severe pain than this seventeen-year-old had known before. There I was, driving home from town in the car my grandfather had given me. It was old, constantly leaking oil, as long as a boat, and near the end of its life. Still, it got me where I needed to go. But that day it died. The billow of smoke from the engine was so thick and tall that the boys playing baseball in the nearby field thought the car was on fire. I drove that car up the gravel driveway, parked it, and never drove it again.

That same day, I got a "Dear John" letter from the girlfriend I'd met on a youth trip and had been writing all summer. Later that evening, I went to my job. I'd been hired to clean a doctor's office. It was fantastic pay and hours, especially for someone still in school. But when I got there that night, I found out the contracting company that hired me had been fired.

In less than ten hours I lost my car, my girlfriend, and my job.

When I got home, I went straight to my mother's bedroom. It was about 10 p.m., and she was sitting up in her bed. I stopped outside her door and angrily demanded, "What kind of prayers are you praying?"

"Boy, I'm not praying for you anymore," she said. "I put you in God's hands."

That scared me. If the events of the day were an example of what it meant to be in God's hands, then I didn't want to be there anymore!

That day changed me, at least partially. I still had to go through some other refining fires, but that was the beginning of change in my life. That incident played a massive part in the process of knocking away my rebellious attitude. When I compare my story to The Rebel of Psalm 107, I recognize how things had to get to a much worse state before he listened. Left unchecked, my rebellious spirit would have landed me in a severe Prison.

It's important to note that rebellion looks different in various situations and can range from light to severe, but the focus here is the spirit of rebellion, however it shows up. The Rebel's consequence is not always physical iron bars. Most of the time, The Rebel's Prison is figurative.

The Bible tells us of several people who ended up in The Rebel's Prison, whether literally or figuratively, because of their insistence on doing evil and rejecting God's ways.

Samson ignored his calling and intentionally rebelled against God's law to please his own passions (Judges 14–16).

King Manasseh despised the godly way he was raised, only wanted to do evil, and became one of the worst sinners of his time (2 Chronicles 33:2).

King Jehoiachin was a teenage king who

committed evil in God's sight. He rebelled against God, against the prophets of God, and against the Babylonian King Nebuchadnezzar (Jeremiah 27).

So how can someone tell if they are in The Rebel's Prison, bound with chains, under hard labor, unable to get free on their own? If they cannot get away from their addictions, their fears, their self-destructive ways, then they are likely in a Prison. They tell themselves that one of these days they'll change, but they can't—at least not on their own. No matter what they do, it always comes back. They may say they love God, but they're in bondage. Their imprisonment may even be hidden from others. No one knows what's binding their lives, yet they live like a captive. A Rebel can be lonely, distant from God, bound by something they can't run away from, always hoping that a new cure will fix their problems, yet constantly falling back into the same place.

Today, most Rebels are bound in a spiritual or mental Prison. These are cages of addiction of the body or the mind, chains of shame, perversions of the heart. These are people enslaved to sin or bound by terrorizing fears. Some have a loss of physical, financial, or relational freedom, and some are in an actual physical prison, living their lives behind metal bars because of their direct rebellion against God. These are Rebels whose chains, visible or invisible, are holding them down, hurting them physically and spiritually. Rebels who are wishing they were free.

But no, my people won't listen.
Israel doesn't want me around.
So I am letting them go their
blind and stubborn way, living
according to their own desires.
But oh, that my people would listen to me!
Oh, that Israel would follow me,
walking in my paths!

Psalm 81:11–13 (TLB)

RETURN

Can you imagine The Rebel alone in his cell, lying on the floor, trying to be comfortable despite his chains? Look at The Prison walls around him, and you'll see carved into the wall multiple plans for how he was going to get out of this place. He tried and tried to find a way to escape, but it always failed. He doesn't believe deliverance is possible anymore. His body shows the marks of his bitter trouble until finally, he can't even stand up.

The Rebel was under such a heavy load that he stumbled and fell. He now lies on the ground with no one coming to help him. No one in The Prison cares. Look closely at the heavy load he's trying to carry, and you'll see regret, shame, brokenness, and guilt. There's no way a person can carry for very long the condemning thoughts, the list of their failures, the roster of people they've hurt, and the weight of their own hopelessness.

The pain of Prison would be enough for most of us to return to the Lord, but not The Rebel. It's horrible to say, but The Rebel needs to fall to the very bottom of their life before they will come back to God. The Rebel in Psalm 107 is put under bondage and suffering. This is the payment, or the result, of sins that once seemed so delightful.

Solomon said that the bread of deceit tastes sweet, but afterward your mouth is filled with gravel (Proverbs 20:17). Who in their right mind would trade a brief, sweet taste of bread for gravel that would fill their mouth? Seemingly nobody, and yet that's exactly the deception of sin. It was the enticement of the forbidden that attracted The Rebel away from the goodness of the Almighty. I can imagine being the once-proud Rebel, who knew better than God, now lying on the cold, wet, unforgiving ground of The Prison they chose, buried under a load of hurt and pain and unable to get up one more time.

What do we do in that situation? What are our options?

There is one:

We can cry out to God in our trouble.

Yes, from right there on the ground, in The Prison, while still captive, we can cry out in our desperate moment of need. Bound up intrinsically in that cry is the idea of repentance. It would be difficult, if not impossible, to honestly cry out to God for his help without asking for his merciful forgiveness. There is not a single passage or verse or story in the Bible where the people got their lives together *before* they turned to God. No Bible story exists that tells of a man who cleaned himself up first and figured out a few things first so he could cry out to God in prayer. No, ma'am. No, sir. Right there in the worst of Prisons, lying in the worst possible conditions, buried under the weight of shame and hurt, we can cry out to him with all our heart. He has promised to hear our cry.

> Then they cried to the LORD in their trouble,
> and he saved them from their distress.
> He brought them out of darkness, the utter darkness,
> and broke away their chains. (Psalm 107:13–14)

Look how God rescued The Rebel in Psalm 107. God led him out of his deep darkness and gloom and snapped those chains. The Rebel was delivered in the nick of time, pulled out by God from that desperate trouble just before he died. How powerful and wonderful God is! He broke down the bronze Prison gates and cut right through the iron bars.

Only God could have orchestrated this Prison break. Friends tried, family members gave up, and everyone thought it useless, but God brought The Rebel out.

— *Warning* —

There is a strange version of bitterness and unforgiveness that the Rebel behind bars must be aware of while waiting for deliverance. It typically isn't a bitterness at God or others. Instead, the Rebel can become bitter toward themself. They know exactly who is at fault, and it is easy to fall into such a place of deep regret and anger at their own stupidity that they don't even believe God will hear them pray.

Constantly reviewing your mistakes and chastising yourself is not the same as crying out to God for help. Be very careful to keep your focus on the only One who can rescue you from this Prison. Don't allow that focus to stay on your past, your failures, or your rebellion. Repent of it and let it go.

Hear the Testimony of The Rebel

I waited patiently for the LORD; and He inclined to me and heard my cry. He also brought me up out of a horrible pit, out of the miry clay, and set my feet upon a rock, and established my steps. He has put a new song in my mouth—Praise to our God; many will see it and fear and will trust in the LORD.

—Psalm 40:1–3, NKJV

*Fools because of their transgression,
and because of their iniquities, are
afflicted. Their soul abhorreth all manner
of meat; and they draw near unto the
gates of death. Then they cry unto the
LORD in their trouble, and he saveth
them out of their distresses. He sent his
word, and healed them, and delivered
them from their destructions. Oh that
men would praise the LORD for his
goodness, and for his wonderful works
to the children of men! And let them
sacrifice the sacrifices of thanksgiving,
and declare his works with rejoicing.*

Psalm 107:17–22

THE FOOL

The way of a fool is right in his own eyes,
but he who heeds counsel is wise.

Proverbs 12:15 (NKJV)

PLAYING WITH FIRE

THE FOOL

Have you ever been so sick that you thought you could feel life gradually leaving your body? Almost to the point of knowing it was the end? I've thought it. I've had plenty of time to think while lying on this sickbed. My only activity, for as long as I can remember, has been rolling over. It's a pathetic attempt to keep my shoulders and hips from developing sores. I can't stop them anymore. I wonder if I will actually see death when it shows up.

I wasn't always a bag of bones, hanging onto life by a couple of loose fingernails. The few friends who have checked on me attempt to hide their shock at how bad I look. Everyone is stunned by how quickly I've changed from extremely active to nearly comatose. It's a strange reality, because my mind is still healthy. I remember how things used to be, imagine that I am still my previously healthy self. I'm still young. I'm not ready to die.

Life used to be normal. And wonderful. I was always into something interesting or entertaining. I enjoyed the world, new things, new people.

Everyone else was too concerned about following rules. Sure, some rules are important, but most of them aren't necessary. I don't see what's so wrong with doing things my own way. Let me be clear, I consider myself a follower of Yahweh. I never wanted to be a rebel. I knew dummies who had turned their backs on God. But not me. God and I are on good terms, and I think he understands my lifestyle.

My buddies would describe me as someone who played with fire. But from my perspective, there wasn't any danger. It was all fun, I was not actually going to get burned.

My friends were my life. Something my mother could not understand. She cornered me in the shop about it one afternoon.

"I'm concerned about the people you're spending your time with. That boy is not right. Something in his heart is wicked. I am telling you, as your mother, he is going to lead you away from God."

It didn't matter how she tried to approach it; my defenses always went up just the same and just as fast.

"You don't trust me at all, do you? I can be friends with someone and not be like them. This is a worthless conversation. You know we've been friends since we were little kids. I'm not leaving him because you're afraid. That's your problem, not mine." I kicked the door as I left, and it broke at the base.

I love my mom, I truly do. But I knew better than

anyone how I wanted to live. It seems like I felt angry with my parents constantly, and I hated my own home. They thought I was being rebellious, but they didn't understand me. I wasn't doing anything wrong. I would never reject the words of God. I wasn't that stupid. I could repeat the Scriptures. And I did good things.

Most of the rules the priests try to push on everyone are ridiculous. God doesn't care about them, and I could prove it.

I grew up being taught that we'd get sick and die from eating the food of the heathen, but I tried it, and it was delicious. And I never got sick. I couldn't justify why we weren't supposed to go to the heathen market; not only was the food great, it was also inexpensive—a win-win in my book.

One time, some scribe from our synagogue saw me chowing down near the Temple meat market. He had a stern warning for me then.

"Young man, God has strictly warned us not to eat the heathen's meat. Do you know for sure that they drained the blood first?"

"I figure it's best not to ask," I said. "There's no way I can be doing the wrong thing if I don't know for sure." I laughed at my own wit.

He definitely didn't think it was funny, but that meat on a stick was delicious. People get all heated about the silliest things. I'm sure he was well-meaning, but what was the big problem with enjoying my lunch?

Another thing. There was a girl I liked for a

while. We spent some intimate time together in secret before I got tired of her and God didn't strike me down. See? So why are we following these antiquated rules if they clearly don't bring punishment?

But the most serious messes I ever got into were usually because of my mouth. Seems that I've always got to have the last word. Once, a few of us were asked to help a widow. We cleaned out her animal pens and rebuilt the ones that were broken down. It was hot, smelly, and dirty work. Somebody came up with the idea that it would be funny if we took one of her lambs and hid it.

"It would be hilarious. She's getting so old that she'd think she lost it. It would be so funny watching her look everywhere trying to remember where she left it." We laughed at the idea.

But one of the younger kids spoke up. "No. Don't do that. Come on, guys. That's cruel, and you know the rules about taking care of widows. Besides, think about how this could look if someone found out. You could really get into a lot of trouble."

I snorted at that. "Here's a better idea. I'll hide the lamb behind our shop. When we're finished with the job, and she comes to look over our work, I'll pretend like there never was a lamb. She won't know what to think!"

The guys I was with laughed and egged me on—except for the boy with the conscience. Why did he have to be so uptight? Besides, it was only a joke. I'd bring it back after a day or so and the widow would be fine. It's not like we were really taking the lamb. No hard feelings, right?

I seriously doubted God cared about some poor widow's lamb. The way I understood God's rules, as long as you eventually did the right thing, then it would all be okay in the end.

I was pretty sure God saw it that way too.

My people are fools;
they do not know me.
They are senseless children;
they have no understanding.
They are skilled in doing evil;
they know not how to do good.

Jeremiah 4:22 (NIV)

THE FALL

THE FOOL

Eventually, something changed in my heart. I can't tell you when it started exactly, but I no longer found pleasure in showing everyone how little the rules mattered. I craved something more. More excitement. More danger. I would never have called myself perverse, but in my honest moments, I knew that some kind of darkness had grown in me. I enjoyed pushing someone else to do something twisted and sick, but I didn't fear the consequences because my hands were clean. If they were caught or beaten, it was their own fault. I had only suggested the idea.

I had figured out in life that it was best to stay out of the spotlight while doing shady things. If you also helped people, everything evened out in the end. So, I worked for them, volunteered to do things I despised, and looked like the best young person in the village. Only a few people knew the real me, but I didn't care what they thought.

I knew I was a good person; it didn't matter to me if they disagreed. Occasionally someone would get in my face and challenge my "wicked ways". I despised well-meaning uncles and interventions from neighbors who attempted to 'save me'. Didn't they realize I was safe enough?

I decided I'd punch the next idiot who told me I was manipulative and deceitful. Hey, I still loved God— just in my own personal way. Plenty of religious people were fakes. I was way better than them. I still attended synagogue, was with my mom for most Sabbaths, and I could recite the evening prayer scriptures.

God understood. Of that I was sure. We had an agreement. I would leave him alone, and he would leave me alone.

But one morning, I woke up and my stomach ached something fierce. It was bad for a few hours and then I threw up. But then it seemed like I was going to be okay and for a couple of weeks I was mostly back to normal.

I spent my days with my friends having a good time until the muscles aches started. I remember waking up with chills in the night and then in the next morning I was covered with sweat. I washed my body, but I was sore for the rest of the day.

Something changed in my mind. I couldn't pretend I wasn't frustrated with everyone like I had in the past. Headaches and pain in my legs and arms stayed with me all day long and I snapped at everyone for every little thing.

My carefully hidden loathing for all the 'common

people' came to the surface. Maybe because the soreness and tiredness worried me or maybe because the pain wouldn't leave. Someone was taking their sweet time with an old cart in front of me, and I yelled at them to get out of my way. It took forever to get to the fence I was trying to repair. The old priest I was supposed to be assisting had trouble hearing me, and I practically bit his head off.

What was going on with me? It was like my most wicked self was clawing out from behind my carefully built walls. And I couldn't cure my headaches.

I gave up on the fence, left it half-finished, and walked back home. Maybe my mom could get me healthy. It was the first time I'd asked for her help in a long while, but I needed her now. She made some concoction with salt, honey, and a few other vile-tasting things, but I knew it would fix me up. I would drink that, sleep it off, and be better by morning.

I got into bed that day and never got out.

Mom tried. She really tried. She used every herb and natural potion she could come up with, but none of them worked. The local doctor came and asked me lots of questions. He'd come by once before and gave me some medicine to try. But it didn't help. Now he listened to my list of symptoms: the chills, the fevers, the headaches, plus some new difficulty breathing and, worst of all, the painful diarrhea.

His mouth tightened as he listened; he nodded his head. "This is clearly a case of worms from eating uncooked meat, likely pork. Have you been eating the food of the pagans, son?"

I wasn't gonna deny it. What would be the point?

He left some powder that I was supposed to mix with water. I could see my mom asking the doctor questions in the other room, but I couldn't make out the words. I didn't need to hear them, though. I saw the shake of his head, the purse of his lips. I saw my mother catch her breath in shock.

She didn't have to tell me what he said. I already knew.

You plunged me into the bottom of the pit,
into dark places,
into the depths.

Psalm 88:7 (CJB)

SICK UNTO DEATH

THE FOOL

Shadows are growing long, and the sun is dipping toward the horizon. The day is ending, and my life is slipping into the pit of death. I can remember a day when I felt free and healthy, but I don't remember how long ago it was. Seems like I've been here forever. So many days and nights have blended into one long, painful, feverish dream.

I confess that I built this Sickbed experience with my own foolishness. It would be a lie to blame anyone else. I can feel the agony of my horrible life choices weighing me down. Why didn't I listen? Why did I think that nothing bad would ever happen to me?

I can see it clearly for the first time in my life. I was headed for death one way or another. If I hadn't gotten sick, I would have continued to do worse and worse because I didn't think consequences would ever find me. Somebody probably would have beaten me to death. Or maybe I would have rotted to death in some jail. Instead, I am living out both of those experiences in my old bedroom, back in the place I vowed to never revisit. I'm bound in a sickness that takes away my freedom as much as any heavy chain, and I'm dying little by little every day. I would rather have been kicked and punched or locked in a cell.

I've tried everything that anyone has asked me to do, but nothing works. I've endured elixirs, special tea, murky water, and quasi-medical visits from people who tried to heal me. Nothing has helped. I can't stand upright without my mom. I can't even get up by myself. And I can barely eat anything. I've lost so much weight and what little muscle I used to have.

Sickness is also a revealer of who your friends are. I suppose I actually have very few, because the old ones have stopped coming by. It shows what a shallow, useless life I lived. People who warned me along the way are probably saying, "I told you so."

Why did I put myself here? This sickness is my fault. I refused to listen to warnings, and I rejected the words of those who loved me—all the while maintaining that I still loved God.

Today something new showed up, a raspy cough that turned to bloody spittle. I can tell my body won't last much longer. Mom has been so kind to me, but I can't stand the sight or smell of food, even her food, though it used to be my favorite. She makes a dish with barley and fish that's heavenly with her fresh bread. I used to enjoy it, but now if I even smell food, my stomach convulses.

And it's worse knowing that it's all because of my

disobedience to God. I'm paying the penalty for playing with evil. I've suffered on this bed for so long that I feel I would be better off dead. Wickedness demands payment. I know it. I'm paying it. I would do anything to change this, to escape this horror I've created for myself. Nothing was worth it. Not one moment of deceitful pleasure or tasting forbidden fruit of activities that I knew from childhood not to touch. This should not be happening to me.

If only I could go back. *God, please give me another chance.* I would listen. I would humble myself. I would leave every wicked friend. Just one day. One pure, free, healthy day to start over. It's all I can think about.

Think. I tried to get my muddled mind to be clear and remember the precious Scripture verses I once studied. I loved God, at least I thought I did, but my life has been wasted. It will soon be over. Nobody can fix me, or deliver me, or pull me out of this inevitable slide into hell.

Oh, for a Healer who could restore me to life again. *O God! Have mercy on my soul.*

The Fool's Prayer

O LORD, don't be angry at me. Have compassion on me, O God. I am very weak and sick. Heal me, O LORD; my bones hurt. If you love me, please deliver me from this death. How long will I be like this? Will you restore me to health? I know you can rescue me. I'm no good for you if I'm dead. LORD, I am so tired of crying and moaning in pain. Hear my plea for help. The LORD is hearing my cry for help. God will answer my prayer.

—Paraphrase of Psalm 6:1–2, 9

*In the thirty-ninth year of his reign
Asa was diseased in his feet—until his
disease became very severe; yet in his
disease he did not seek the LORD,
but relied on the physicians.*

2 Chronicles 16:12 (AMPC)

ANCIENT HEALTHCARE

The sick of the ancient world in which the Old Testament was written had limited options for relief. There were no hospitals for the general populace. A king could procure special medical treatment and care like we might expect from a hospital setting, but the most common approaches involved herbs and naturally derived remedies. And the ancient Israelites had numerous natural remedies as a first line of defense against sickness. These remedies were appropriate for less-severe physical ailments. A sore throat, for example, could be soothed with hot water, lemon, and honey. The mandrake root was used as a fertility treatment in Genesis 30:14–15, and a soothing balm from Gilead is referenced in Jeremiah 8:22.

The most common diseases were of the eye and ear. Many physical disabilities also resulted from war or accidental injury. A whole chapter in the Bible is devoted to a wide range of skin problems, including possibly vitiligo and ringworm (Leviticus 13). Isaiah 10:16 speaks of "a wasting sickness" that afflicted

Assyria's strong warriors. Priests and Levites were given regulations on how to deal with certain infections and molds (Leviticus 11–14). The people in those times lived in an environment surrounded by blowing dust, dirt, contaminated food, impure water, city and town sewage, refuse, and garbage. And animals that potentially carried disease and various sicknesses could be found in every village.

Physicians are sometimes mentioned in the Bible. Occasionally they're mentioned with negative connotations, but not because God didn't want the people to use natural remedies. After all, he is the mastermind behind the healing benefits of plants. Rather, the writers indicate that God wanted his people to call on his help first—before calling for a doctor. God wanted them to trust in him more than any potion or physician.

Prayer to God was always the right thing to do and should have been the first option. But sometimes people, like King Asa in 2 Chronicles 16, insisted on trying everything but God. He refused to seek the Lord, and he died because of his diseased feet. The prophet Hanani came to this king and told him that he had acted foolishly because he did not rely on the Lord his God. Hanani relayed to him that God was dissatisfied with his foolish choices, and from that point on, he would always have wars. Upon hearing this, King Asa was so angry that he put the prophet in prison and began to abuse the people of Israel.

We don't know exactly what The Fool did to contract the Sickness that left him barely alive.

Psalm 107:17 only tells us that he suffered because of the evil he had indulged in. His crimes and guilty deeds produced suffering, and he despised all food. As he was unable to eat, his condition only got worse, and he felt close to death.

Many sick people in the Bible did not suffer because of some wicked act or evil thing they had done. Sometimes it was a tainted food source or a widespread illness, and directions were passed down in the Law of Moses for these types of situations. Once, many at the school of the prophets with Elisha became deathly ill when someone unwittingly gathered up poisonous gourds to add to the stew. They didn't willfully bring this on themselves, and they would have died without intervention.

But that was not the case with The Fool.

This Sickness was entirely his fault, and he knew it.

*Fools mock at sin, but among
the upright there is favor.*

Proverbs 14:9 (NIV)

THE MIND OF THE FOOL

There are different kinds of Fools found throughout the Bible. The Fool in Psalm 107 is the Silly Fool. He is not The Rebel, who knew exactly what he should do and refused to do it. He is simply a foolish person, continually putting himself in danger because he never thought the consequences would reach him. His foolishness has a core of moral waywardness, even perversity. His life before he was struck down with this horrible Sickness was one of satisfying his fleshy impulses and living it up.

The Rebel and Fool do have something in common: Their pain was caused by their own choices. The Rebel, in a sense, built his own Prison. And The Fool created his own Sickbed.

But unlike The Rebel, who looked right in the face of those who warned him, refused to listen, and intentionally committed evil, The Fool truly and naïvely thought he could avoid the consequences of sin. The Fool believed he was better than The Rebel. In some twisted way, he assumed that he could both enjoy himself and be a good follower of Yahweh.

Both characters were totally to blame for their own Distress, and in the end they knew it. Everyone who reads their stories clearly sees that they caused their own pain and heartache.

The Fool was looking to have a good time in life, and some of his highest enjoyment was ignoring the rules. It seemed fine for him to do things he wasn't supposed to, and he loved the thrill of crossing a line. He knew better than everyone else about any topic. All you had to do was ask him, and he'd tell you. The rules didn't really apply to The Fool, they were there for other people. He was confident that he wouldn't get into trouble. His way of life did not respect danger; he was invincible.

If someone tried to redirect or rebuke him, The Fool was unreasonable. He was full of arrogance and proud of his reasoning—more dumb than rebellious.

When people talked reason to The Fool, he partially listened. But he was proud of the loopholes he found. In his twisted mentality, he was doing things his way while living as a believer at the same time. He could point to times when he prayed and repented or diligently read the Scriptures. God never seemed to mind when he decided the rules didn't apply to him. This self-justifying mindset kept him from truly receiving godly wisdom and direction. "I did it my way" would have been his theme song.

The Fool's mouth always got him into trouble.

When things went wrong, he became very angry. He believed he was always right, and he reacted with disdain to anything contrary. He was also infatuated with wickedness because he didn't experience it growing up. To him, things that were off-limits or that had been labeled immoral or dangerous were an enticing treat.

One scary thing about The Fool is that some of the things he said were correct, especially when he talked about God. But this gave him a false sense that he was always right about everything.

If you met The Fool today, you might think that he's a mature Christian. He may appear as someone who shows up at events, goes to church, and is involved in the typical activities of a believer. His foolishness is hidden—except when he's talking; that's when he reveals himself.

Out of the heart, the mouth speaks. (Luke 6:45)

What should we do if we recognize in ourselves some of these same mentalities and behaviors? Do we delude ourselves into thinking we're okay? Are we acting ignorantly about life and always attempting to slip past trouble?

The Fool didn't despise God or God's Word. He just thought he'd always be able to stiff-arm consequences because nothing had ever caught up with him before. It was a very short-sighted view of life because the only facts he would consider were those from his own experiences. He could meet ten people who struggled in their lives because of foolishness but would disregard their personal testimonies because the consequences hadn't happened to him. At least not yet.

But by the end of the story his stubborn resistance melted away. Now it was clear to him that he had been foolish. He would have done anything to get out of that bed and walk into the sunshine. He would be humble. He would listen. He would draw a new line of right and wrong in his heart and build a fence in his life against evil temptations, so he could forever stay away from those corrupting sins that brought him down. How sad to think that he finally understood the importance of what his parents taught him, but now it was too late.

We can clearly see the suffering that awaited The Fool. It was inevitable.

God is so kind to send us messages, warnings, stop signs, and pleadings to get us to turn back to him. But never forget that God is not a man who could be confused by any hidden wickedness. He knows all. He sees our hearts and is trying to keep us from The Fool's punishment.

This story provides us with a cautionary tale and begs us to ask ourselves: Am I The Fool? Have I acted like him?

I identify with some of the mentalities of The Foolish man, especially in my past. I have family members and friends who echoed some of these concerns and warnings—but they were about me. It's a gut-wrenching feeling to look back on my life and remember those times of feeling invincible, as though the heartaches and troubles of life would never happen to me.

I have been blessed to be raised by optimistic parents, and I love to look at life in the best possible light. However, there is a fine line between optimism and foolishness.

A prudent person foresees danger and takes precautions. The simpleton goes blindly on and suffers the consequences. (Proverbs 27:12, NLT)

The simpleton is similar to The Fool. I have been that guy, thinking I was being optimistic, when in reality I was being foolish. Wisdom is seeing the pain other people are experiencing and determining to live differently. Foolishness is seeing the same pain and telling yourself it doesn't apply to you.

It hurts me to write this because with this crazy mindset I have caused trouble for myself and for those I loved. God had to take me through the School of Hard Knocks before I could learn this simple lesson.

I have either said these words or heard others close to me say something like them: "It's not a big deal. I love the Lord. He knows. It's just that I don't think this is a problem for me." But those words will lead to regret. They did in my life and in the lives of those I love.

The truth is that we all will fail, mess up, and

experience trauma in this life. This is normal and to be expected. Yet the pain will be much worse for someone who insists on blindly walking through life. We need to pray that God will open our eyes to the fallacy of The Fool.

––––

A friend told me his story, the testimony of his life, of when he acted like The Fool in Psalm 107.

When he was a teen, his father pastored a small, growing church.

This pastor's son always had an ornery streak, but his desire for trouble really showed up when he started driving. On Sundays, he was involved in his father's church, but during his free time throughout the week, he was driving around with his friends looking for trouble. He flippantly brushed off all the warnings from his parents and other well-meaning people in the church.

One day while out messing around in his truck, he was broadsided at a four-way stop. A car smashed in his driver's side door, and they rushed him to the hospital for emergency surgery. It should have been the perfect wake-up call, but even that wasn't enough.

After surviving the crash and recovering so quickly, he felt invincible. He believed nothing could stop him. He even began to drive his truck at full speed through intersections.

All this time, he continued to play the part of a

"good Christian young man" for anyone who was looking. His life revolved around church, and he fooled himself into believing that the things he did didn't matter because he was still a good person.

The Lord directed his praying parents to step down from pastoring that church, and his father, following the Lord's hand for the salvation of his son, moved their family to a bigger city where they joined a large church. It was that massive intervention that changed the trajectory of my friend's life.

In a moment, he felt he had lost everything—his local prestige, his friends, and eventually his truck. He felt as though his life was over and that he would never recover to be the person he once was.

Then he met a young lady who stole his heart. Seeing her godly life caused him to reflect on his own. A girl like that would be looking for a godly man. He recognized that he was not that man. Her positive pressure acted as a wakeup call for him and at last he clearly saw the change he needed in his life. Because of her influence, he began to have a relationship with Jesus for himself.

His life was forever changed because of the mercy of God and his parents' willingness to do whatever it took.

———

Consider these verses to understand the inherent difficulties of The Fool:

"If a wise man has a controversy with a foolish and arrogant man, The foolish man [ignores logic and fairness and] only rages or laughs, and there is no peace (rest, agreement)." (Proverbs 29:9, AMP).

This fool is the same as The Fool in our story from Psalm 107. It doesn't matter what the wise man says. The Fool cannot or will not hear him.

"Counsel in the heart of man is like deep water, but a man of understanding will draw it out" (Proverbs 20:5, NKJV).

This person, the "man of understanding," can meet with the same wise man in the previous verse and walk away with precious counsel or insight. The Fool hears an argument, the man of understanding hears good counsel.

Unfortunately, these words cannot help a Fool until they are hurting, in pain, and desperate for a change. But we don't have to get next to the "gates of death" before we listen to wise instructions from God's Word. A little pain might be enough to get our attention. I pray that it will.

King David sang this funeral song for Abner. "Did Abner die like a fool?"

2 Samuel 3:33 (NCV)

DEATH VALLEY

When did The Fool realize that this Sickness wasn't going away or that he would never get better? Because of his foolishness, he refused to believe that he wouldn't recover. His mindset didn't change until he was close to the end.

I imagine his poor mother gave him water to drink, helped him get up to use the toilet, cleaned him when he vomited, sat by his bed, and wiped the sweat from his face with a cool rag. He didn't know what was wrong with his body, but he knew he was on the edge of death. Countless times The Fool would have wished he were already dead.

I wonder, when did he cry out to God? We know why he waited. It was because he couldn't believe that he would not be able to get out of this pit. He had lived his life sidestepping trouble. They always said it would catch up to him one day, and it finally did. Can you imagine facing certain destruction, while knowing that you're in this pit because of your own foolishness?

Healing was impossible through any natural means. Many had tried and failed to restore his health. The last physician told his mother that nothing more could be done to save her boy. It was time to make him as comfortable as possible and wait for the end. Word had spread, and funeral preparations were already being made. His tomb was open and prepared to receive his wasted body. Everybody had given up. Only God could heal him.

This was the moment he had to cry out to God for help. Of course, any time during his Sickness would have been the right moment to ask God for deliverance. Unfortunately, most people who are like The Fool will not ask God for help or turn away from their sinful lives until this final moment—just before death. And some, like King Asa, never repent or humble themselves before God (2 Chronicles 16:12–13). To do so would be to admit that they were wrong, and Fools never think they are wrong. That's the main characteristic of The Fool.

Read how God rescued The Fool in Psalm 107 verse 20. He sent his word and healed The Fool. What a powerful Word God has! His Word alone can heal you.

> He sent His word, and healed them, and delivered them from their destructions. (Psalm 107:20, NKJV)

God delivered The Fool while he had one foot in the grave. God pulled him out in the nick of time, saving him from death's doorstep. Thank God for his mercy and for his incredible love for even his most foolish children. There is healing available from heaven—physical, mental, and spiritual recovery for our lives. God is true to his Word.

This message hurts when it hits because we tend to hold tightly to our pain. We insist on doing things our own way and kick back at God's mercy and messages of warning. However, I would rather be right with God and sick in my body than healthy and far from God. I say this because I know people who have recovered or been healed but then strayed from God after his deliverance.

God loves us enough to discipline us and allow pain in our lives in order to turn us away from foolishness. He is never a bad father, never spiteful. He will not injure someone innocent in our life to get our attention. Yet he is willing to use or allow many things to reach us and save us from our foolishness.

God promises to hear the prayer of the hungry and broken. We must remember that God heals in his own way, not necessarily in our way. He can do it miraculously or supernaturally, through medicine, over time, or through wise counsel. He can even heal us eternally by taking us home to be with him in glory.

— *Warning* —

People can die because they have given up. When hope is gone from someone with a serious illness, life usually does not stay around long. The Fool in our story was sick unto death, and if you are in a similar situation, you must keep hope alive. The Lord is the only One who can answer your cry, and he can deliver you from the grip of death. Focus on him, his Holy Word, and not on the physical senses. God is able to do whatever is necessary to rescue you.

Hear the Testimony of The Fool

I waited patiently for the LORD; he turned to me and heard my cry. He lifted me out of the slimy pit, out of the mud and mire; he set my feet on a rock and gave me a firm place to stand. He put a new song in my mouth, a hymn of praise to our God. Many will see and fear the LORD and put their trust in him.

—Psalm 40:1–3, NIV

From the end of the earth I will cry to
You, when my heart is overwhelmed;
lead me to the rock that is higher than I.

Psalm 61:2 (NKJV)

THE SOLUTION

*Then all the disciples
deserted him and fled.*

Matthew 26:56b (NIV)

THREE REACTIONS TO A DISTRESS

Seasons of Distress are common experiences that everyone has or will encounter at some point in their life. Some of us have faced more than one: The Wilderness, The Storm, The Prison, or The Sickbed.

People typically react one of three ways to the troubles they face. We can see these reactions played out in the actions of the disciples after Jesus was arrested. If we overlay Matthew 26, Luke 22, and John 19, we'll see that John stayed with Jesus, Peter walked at a distance behind the Roman guards, and everyone else—aside from Judas Iscariot—ran away.

These are still the three basic reactions we see among followers of Jesus when they find themselves in Distress today.

Unfortunately, there are always those who run away from the Lord when they're in severe Distress. Trouble comes and they decide they can't handle it. They didn't expect it to happen like this. The trouble or pain is too great, and they conclude they can't trust God anymore. They're done. They're out. These people struggle the most with feeling that God doesn't make sense. They reason that if God truly cared, he wouldn't let this happen to them. They end up slipping or backing away from the Lord.

But the good news is that the story doesn't have to be over for anyone who struggles with their faith. Those same nine scared disciples recovered after Jesus was resurrected. When we repent, he will forgive us. He will not leave us because he is faithful and can't be untrue to himself (see 2 Timothy 2:13).

Simon Peter didn't run, but neither did he stay by the Lord's side after his failed attempt to single-handedly fight what could have been as many as 600 Roman soldiers, officers from the chief priests, and Pharisees. He represents the second choice many believers have in serious trouble: "Peter followed him at a distance" (Matthew 26:58a, NKJV).

We're typically like Simon Peter when we first start walking with the Lord. Our new faith is exciting, up close, and personal. We feel confident in our relationship with Jesus. But when we're confronted by terrifying fear in a dark period of life—the way Peter was when confronting soldiers, swords, betrayal, and confusion—it can cause us, like Peter, to hang back. It was one thing for Peter to proclaim he would never betray the Lord while sitting together at a supper, but quite a different story when in the middle of the action.

Peter declared, "Even if everyone else deserts you, I will never desert you."

Jesus replied, "I tell you the truth, Peter—this very night, before the rooster crows, you will deny three times that you even know me."

"No!" Peter insisted. "Even if I have to die with you, I will never deny you!" And all the other disciples vowed the same. (Matthew 26:33–35, NLT)

Similar to Peter, those who follow Jesus at a distance now will likely deny him later. This type of believer seems to stay around, still going through the motions even in the midst of trouble, but something has changed inside. Friends might say they're not the same after a Storm. They still believe in God, but there's a deep pain, and they've lost their simple faith and trust in him. Peter continued to stay distant from the Lord, and when confronted later as he warmed his hands over a fire, he even pretended that he didn't know who Jesus was.

Finally, we see the reactions of those who refuse to let go of the Lord during the worst of their problems. John the Beloved stayed close despite not understanding. He did not know what to do, but he stayed. This is the best scenario, though it can be the most difficult. John stayed close, and he risked putting himself in danger by his loyalty to his master.

Earlier in his ministry, Jesus said some confusing things without any explanation. It was not a Distress or severe trouble, but for the crowds who followed Jesus, it was still so difficult to hear that most of them left. He called himself the Living Bread and said that eating his flesh was necessary for eternal life. It didn't make sense to them. They had no idea why he would say something diametrically opposite to the words of Moses. The people knew that *had* to be wrong; nearly everyone quit following him.

> When many of his disciples heard this, they said, "This is a difficult and harsh and offensive statement. Who can [be expected to] listen to it?" (John 6:60, AMP)

> Jesus said to the twelve, "Do you also want to go away?" (John 6:67 NKJV)

While the disciples had no idea what was going on or what Jesus meant by those strange words, they knew his character and trusted him. They knew what they had seen: his miracles, his merciful kindness to the least of society, his teaching and its effects.

Simon Peter was the spokesman for the group, and he answered for them all: "Lord, to whom shall we go? You have the words of eternal life. Also, we have come to believe and know that You are the Christ, the

Son of the living God" (John 6:68–69, NKJV). It's worth noting that Peter was able to do the right thing during *this* difficulty, but he made the wrong choice on the night of the arrest about a year later.

Jesus was the Messiah. The disciples knew he was the One. Staying close to Jesus was the best choice even in the worst times.

Simon had rightly said, "Lord, to whom shall we go?" Simon could be asking us that same question while we are experiencing our worst Distress. "Where shall we go?" Can this world heal our misery? Will The Distress be enough to force us away from Jesus? Will we turn our back on him because of it?

The Bible mentions a church that chose the middle ground. Jesus addresses these believers through the Revelation given to John. The Lord commends the church in Ephesus for their perseverance but then says this:

> Nevertheless, I have this against you, that you
> have left your first love. (Revelation 2:4, NKJV)

Did they stumble when they encountered unexpected heartache or difficulty while following Jesus? I wonder if they lost their first love because of some excruciating issue or if it was a gradual slipping away. We don't know what caused it, but we know the Lord rebuked them for it. Somewhere along their path of following Jesus, they let some distance grow between them and their Lord. Here a little, there a little. Sometimes the misery of a thousand tiny cuts can be as devastating as a shocking emergency room trauma. This is exactly the problem with trying to stay somewhere in the middle between leaving and staying. Nothing works out well for the believer who hangs back.

We may not be able to anticipate Distress, but we can decide how close we will be to Jesus when it hits.

Regardless of which reaction we choose, we may find ourselves saying similar things: "I don't understand," or "Why is God letting this happen?" When we are in a Distress or battling through intense pain, we might be trying to figure out what's going on or what God is doing. We must not let go during this time of extreme confusion and hurt. Letting go of the Lord or becoming distant from him won't get us the answers we seek. The only thing we can do is to stay. We *must* hang on.

One way or another, this Distress will pass.

God loves us.

He knows exactly what is happening in our lives.

He has not lost sight of us or misplaced us.

We must remember that he has a plan.

We only need trust him.

Who shall separate us from the love of Christ? Shall . . . distress?

Romans 8:35a (NKJV)

DISTRESS CHECKLIST

Distress is listed among the seven things the Apostle Paul offers as examples of what might divide us from the love of Christ. Distress as used in this verse indicates a narrow place or, metaphorically, a dire calamity or extreme affliction.

Are you currently in one of these four Distresses? How can you tell? What are clues that the psalmist gives under the inspiration of the Holy Spirit?

— *Wanderers in the Wilderness* —

Walking and wandering look similar from the outside. The main difference is whether the walker is progressing with purpose. The Wanderer is not sure how to get where they need to go. Those who wander often describe their situation as "going through a dry season" or "being unsure of what God is doing in my life."

The Israelites wandered in The Wilderness for roughly thirty-eight years, which meant they were going in circles the whole time. The Lord told Moses, "You have circled this mountain long enough; turn northward" (Deuteronomy 2:3, AMP). They wandered as a result of their disbelief in God's promise and their disobedience to his direction. They lacked faith in God and rebelled against instruction.

The Wanderer in Psalm 107 ended up wandering even though he was doing a good thing. He left Babylon behind and was heading to Jerusalem to be with the people of God. He wasn't rebelling against God, either by thoughts or by actions. One day he was walking and the next he found himself wandering.

Talk to Wanderers today and they'll tell you they love the Lord. Nothing has changed in their faith. They read their Bibles, pray, attend services, yet they feel that they are only going through the motions. The Wandering exist in a world of uncertainty, confusion, and the plodding sensation of putting one foot in front of the other.

— *Sailors in the Storm* —

It's usually evident when someone is in a Storm. Although Storms can have different intensities and lengths, they typically arrive the same way: suddenly and without warning, usually while going about life. No one goes through a Storm without losing something. "We took such a violent battering from the storm that the next day they began to throw the cargo overboard" (Acts 27:18 NIV).

Everyone has at some time been, or will be, The Sailor. Generally speaking, we all live with some combination of job, family, home, routine, to-do lists, demands, and expectations. These things encompass our existence. One could be in the grocery store, asleep in bed, or at church when the next storm hits. If we could prevent a storm, we would. Storms have many causes, they're not our fault, and no one can escape them. The Bible says these things—Storms—are common to man.

Storms can be about finances, relationships, work, health, injury, a loved one's moral failure, or physical death. Of course, we can bring trouble on our own head, like The Rebel and The Fool, but The Storms described here happen *to* us, not *because of* us.

Storms are shocking, fearful, monstrous things that can shake a person's faith and compel them to call for prayer. If someone is asking everyone in their life to pray, it could be an indicator that they're facing a Storm.

— *Rebels in Prison* —

A physical prisoner loses their freedom, and the worst offenders have the least physical freedom. Spiritual imprisonment reflects physical imprisonment. Things like addictions, addictive behaviors, fear, worry, and unforgiveness can bind a person more tightly than physical handcuffs or shackles.

If we cannot tell ourselves no or keep our word to ourselves, then we might be on the pathway to Prison. When we feel bound in our spirit, unable to listen to the Word of God, or frozen while others are worshipping the Lord, we might be in a spiritual Prison.

The Rebel can often end up in a physical prison, but there are also many other kinds of Prisons in life. They may be hopeless conditions or impossible situations we create because our refusal to listen to God and to the warnings we hear from people he sends our way.

Our Prisoner in this story was at the bottom of his existence, completely hopeless. No human being had the power to set him free. Only God could deliver him from his afflictions and tormentors. All The Rebel needed to do was cry out.

But torment is a normal characteristic of an imprisoned Rebel. They may try to control their fierce anger, but instead of turning to God the next time something goes wrong, they lose their temper again.

The Rebel might say, "I can stop anytime I want," or "I'm not hurting anyone," but they typically hit rock bottom before they are willing to change. The Rebel who was a Prisoner in the psalm could not do anything other than reach out to God. There were no more steps he could take to remedy his situation, no change of heart or attitude that would have broken him free, no natural ability that could have delivered him. The time for human solutions had passed.

— *Fools Sick Unto Death* —

This kind of Fool genuinely believes that they love God and aren't doing anything wrong. Or at least they're not as bad as other people. We can identify that we are The Fool when we try to justify our sins. The Fool may persist in the activities or behaviors even after having been warned and rebuked.

Listen to The Fool talk and you'll hear things like, "I understand that it's a problem for others, but it's not that big a deal to me," "Nothing bad can happen to me," or "Everyone believes different things. I'm just not convicted about it."

Proverbs 1:7 tells us that Fools despise wisdom and instruction. This blatant contempt is an indicator that someone is being a Fool. They hate when someone sits them down and tells them how they should do something. Solomon specifically refers to this kind of Fool in Proverbs 12:15 (NKJV). "The way of a fool is right in his own eyes, but he who heeds counsel is wise."

The end of that verse is telling. The Fool will not listen.

From God's perspective, we can draw a pathway from The Fool straight to their destruction. In our story, Sickness has sapped the strength of The Fool as he lies on his bed, struggling to survive. He is past the point of turning around. His only hope is a miracle.

We are headed in that direction if we refuse to

humble ourselves and obey what God wants us to do. Although foolish people may end up on The Sickbed, their judgment is not limited to Sickness. Fools can destroy their lives, their relationships with family and friends, or tear apart their own homes.

> The wise woman builds her house, but with her own hands the foolish one tears hers down. (Proverbs 14:1, NIV)

Solomon wrote of those who refused to listen to wise instruction and direction. It is a desperate picture, filled with the agony of foolish choices.

> "At the end of your life, you will groan when your flesh and body are spent. You will say, 'How I hated discipline! How my heart spurned correction! I would not obey my teachers or turn my ear to my instructors'" (Proverbs 5:11–13, NIV).

What is the solution for The Wanderer, The Sailor, The Rebel, and The Fool? Each of the characters has one thing available to them, one last hope, one thing left they can do to find relief from their Distress: Cry out to the Lord.

In my distress I called upon the LORD, and cried out to my God; He heard my voice from His temple, and my cry came before Him, even to His ears.

Psalm 18:6 (NKJV)

O LORD, how long will you forget me? Forever? How long will you look the other way? How long must I struggle with anguish in my soul, with sorrow in my heart every day? How long will my enemy have the upper hand? Turn and answer me, O LORD my God!

Psalm 13:1–3a (NLT)

CRYING OUT

I've done my best to explain the problems that we all face in our walk with God. I've spent a lot of time outlining the four different kinds of Distress we can get into. Now would be the moment for me to spring the answer. After all, you don't write a book about how to get out of a mess without some clear instructions on how to do so.

And yet I find myself at this crucial point without a particularly good answer. I've read through this psalm in many versions of the Bible. I've searched more than a dozen commentaries. I've prayed about it. I've asked God what these characters said when they prayed.

The same direction showed up time and time again: Cry Out.

But that seemed too simplistic, so I kept searching for a better answer.

It was during that search that the Lord reminded me of a verse in Hosea.

In Hosea 4:6a, the prophet wrote this cry from God: "My people are destroyed from lack of knowledge" (NIV). What kind of knowledge were they lacking? In the rest of the verse, Hosea clearly says they have ignored God's Word and his ways.

In our contemporary world, what knowledge could we possibly be lacking? Especially in this day of hyper-available information, it couldn't be a lack of breaking news or sports statistics. Certainly not the endless stream of how-to videos showing us how to build a deck, plant a garden, improve our health, get rich, or tie a bowtie. The only important information we're missing is the same as what the early Israelites were missing—knowledge of God and his ways, his instruction for how to handle times of Distress.

Why does "Crying Out" matter? Because if we don't, we will continue in our pain; we will stay in our Wilderness, Storm, Prison, or Sickness. No one cries out to God unless they realize how desperately they need him.

In the Gospel of Mark, a blind man sat begging by the roadside in the city of Jericho. He was begging because it was the only way he could survive. A crowd gathered in excitement at a new arrival, and the blind man asked those around him about all the hubbub. He learned that the excitement was about the arrival of Jesus, the teacher from Nazareth who healed people.

As he pondered his circumstance, the blind man realized that if he wanted to get to the teacher, he had only one option. He knew he would not be able to feel his way through the crowd to find Jesus. He also knew that if he waited for the commotion to die down, and Jesus passed by, it would be too late.

So he cried out, "Jesus! Jesus, thou son of David. Have mercy on me!" (Mark 10:47).

The people around Jesus said, "Be quiet, Bartimaeus. You are out of place, and your yelling keeps us from hearing the rabbi." But he would not keep quiet. He cried out until Jesus stopped everything and came to him. There was only one phrase he knew to say. And he wouldn't stop saying it. *"Son of David, have mercy on me!"* Over and over, he shouted out his simple cry for help to the only person who could help him, the only One who could rescue him.

Each of our four characters in Psalm 107 eventually cried out to God. In each scenario—long before they cried out to the One who could deliver them—it became obvious that no human on Earth would be able to rescue or even help them. Yet from their stories it seems that they waited until the last possible moment to cry out to God.

Why did they wait so long to cry out?

Maybe they didn't think their situation was that bad. If these four characters were like us, they might have waited so long because they were stubborn and hadn't yet reached rock bottom. For many of us, it takes a long time and deep pain before we arrive at the end of our self-dependency. Only then do most of us cry out to God.

Maybe they tried the normal human options that

people do when they are in serious trouble. Did The Wanderer convince himself that in a few days he'd find the city? Did The Sailor attempt to steer out of The Storm or think that throwing things overboard would be enough? Did The Rebel plead with the guards or attempt a Prison break? Did The Fool ignore the signs of his Sickness, pretending it would eventually go away and he'd feel better soon?

The author of this psalm leaves out much information, and there are many unanswered questions that I wonder about, especially in how to apply this message to my own life.

How did they cry out? How long? What exactly did they say? Did their cry involve a prayer outline? Perhaps first addressing God, then worshiping, repenting, asking for help, before thanking and praising him ahead of time? And how long did it take God to answer? Did he let the people in Psalm 107 cry out for a while? Or did he begin to answer before they understood that he had heard and was already acting in their situation, just as he did with Jonah? When Jonah cried from the belly of the fish, God told the fish to take Jonah to the shore. It doesn't say that God said a word to Jonah while he was in the fish.

This doesn't mean that you should pray once, then sit in a corner until you hear from God. This is crying out from a place of deep pain that doesn't stop until God moves in your situation. Take every action that the Lord leads you to take. Do everything God wants you to do and what you know is right to do. It is in God's character to rescue us from our Distress—but he will wait for us to cry out to him.

What does it mean to cry out? Why did God leave out the specifics of what the four characters said to him when they cried out for help? We cannot find any specific words they used to cry out to him. Authors intentionally leave things out of their manuscripts if they want you to pay attention to something else. But doesn't God want us to know how to do something correctly, especially if it is the most important part of the story?

Surely, God, you have something specific for those in The Wilderness to pray that's different from that of The Sailor facing a killer Storm. And what about The Rebel? What type of cry should those who are in a Prison of their own making say to you? And The Fool? What should those who are on a Sickbed of their own foolishness cry out? Each of the four should have a specific prayer, right?

Could it be that our cry to God has nothing to do with having the correct prayer posture or the perfect words? It seems that the cry in this psalm is intentionally left ambiguous, because the *act* of crying out is more important than what we say and how we do it. It's personal. There are no perfectly scripted words, no pattern or correct outline. The cry must be from our heart to be genuine before the Lord. God wants us to throw our complete trust into his ability to rescue us, and not in our ability to pray good prayers or barter successfully with him. We should not stop crying out to him or believing that he has heard and is in the process of acting on our behalf. We should cry out to him, knowing that he hears and answers prayer.

The answers I found to my "Cry Out" questions are so simple they appear childish.

Casting all your care on him, for he careth for you. (1 Peter 5:7)

Casting in this verse refers to flinging without regard for where it lands. So go ahead: Toss your cares toward him. God never stops caring for us. It isn't a one-and-done. We haven't wasted our chance for God to care for us. He cares intensely and keeps on caring. God knows the answers to our questions. He sees our tears and hears our cries. He loves us and will come to our rescue when we cry out to him.

Again and again, the same simple answer shows up in this passage of Psalm 107: Cry Out.

I can't think of anything more humbling, childlike, and sheep-like than simply crying out.

Crying Out
Crying Out is not proud, it's humble.
Crying Out is not postured or measured.
Crying Out is uncomfortable and interrupting.
Crying Out is not later, at a more convenient time and place.

Crying Out is now, here.
Crying Out stops life as normal.
Crying Out gets God's attention.

It's simple, personal, and full of emotion because we understand that we desperately need the Lord's help. He is the only One who can rescue us, pull us out of the pit, and bring us into that place of healing.

*He delivers and rescues, and He works
signs and wonders in heaven and
on earth, who has delivered Daniel
from the power of the lions.*

Daniel 6:27 (NKJV)

DELIVERANCE

In Psalm 107, God responded to the cry of each character and crafted a rescue specific to their individual needs. The Fool was healed, The Rebel was saved, The Wanderer was delivered, and The Sailor was brought out.

He led The Wanderer out by the right way so he might go to a city to live; he satisfied his longing, and filled his hungry soul with goodness.

> He led them by a straight way
> to a city where they could settle.
> Let them give thanks to the LORD for his unfailing love
> and his wonderful deeds for mankind,
> for he satisfies the thirsty
> and fills the hungry with good things. (Psalm 107:7–9, NIV)

He calmed The Storm for The Sailor and made the waves still. The quietness brought relief to The Sailor. God guided him to his desired port, the harbor he hoped to reach. When the people assemble, The Sailor will give God worship, blessing the Lord with high praises.

> He stilled the storm to a whisper;
> the waves of the sea were hushed.
> They were glad when it grew calm,
> and he guided them to their desired haven.
> Let them give thanks to the LORD for his
> unfailing love
> and his wonderful deeds for mankind.
> Let them exalt him in the assembly of the people
> and praise him in the council of the elders. (Psalm
> 107:29–32, NIV)

God brought The Rebel out of darkness and gloom, leading him out of Prison, breaking the chains in pieces. He shattered the bronze gates and cut the bars of iron in half so no one could be a prisoner in that place again.

> He brought them out of darkness, the utter
> darkness,
> and broke away their chains.
> Let them give thanks to the LORD for his
> unfailing love
> and his wonderful deeds for mankind,
> for he breaks down gates of bronze
> and cuts through bars of iron. (Psalm 107:14–16
> NIV)

God sent The Fool his word and healed him, rescuing him from the grave. Let him offer sacrifices of thanksgiving and sing joyfully about God's mighty works.

> He sent out his word and healed them;
> he rescued them from the grave.
> Let them give thanks to the LORD for his
> unfailing love
> and his wonderful deeds for mankind.
> Let them sacrifice thank offerings
> and tell of his works with songs of joy. (Psalm
> 107:20–22, NIV)

Do these varied descriptions of God's rescue mean that God will prevent the pain from ever happening? Will he erase The Wilderness wandering? Will he rewind The Storm as though it never happened, gathering back all the materials and supplies lost overboard? Will God jump back in time before the pain of The Prison and stop The Rebel from being rebellious? Will he undo the Sickness and keep The Fool from making bad decisions?

No, he will not. He doesn't always take away the bad, but he will bring good out of the bad. The memories and the scars may remain, but his healing can take away the pain.

Jesus tells us in Luke 10:19, "Behold, I give you the authority to trample on serpents and scorpions, and over all the power of the enemy, and nothing shall by any means hurt you."

The AMPC version says that "nothing shall in any way harm you."

"Harm" in the Bible doesn't always mean the same physical hurt we would think of when defining the word. If that were so, someone should've let the early church know, because they surely didn't get the memo! Those Christians were persecuted, jailed, beaten, and chased from their homes. Stephen was stoned to death, and James lost his head—literally. Jesus told them not to fear those who can kill the body but rather to be concerned about their souls (Matthew 10:28).

It is important, therefore, to understand that God's rescue missions take many forms. He can quiet The Storm around us. He can heal a broken body. He can deliver someone from painful shackles and set them free from Prison. But God can also be with them in The Prison, as he was with Paul. From God's perspective, the ultimate rescue is for us to be in heaven with him. It might seem like a cop-out to say that Sickness and pain will ultimately be resolved by a heavenly, perfect eternity. But it's true.

God is a Deliverer. Someone's present captivity may be so horrible that they can't imagine being free. But be assured that God delivers and has a powerful track record of releasing prisoners. Jesus came and proclaimed that he would set the captive free. God can bring us out in ways that we cannot understand. He has set prisoners free in their spirit and mind, even while they still serve out the days of their physical prison sentence. We can trust him to do the work he delights in accomplishing.

He is a Healer. Jesus paid for our physical healing, but can heal so much more than just our bodies. He can heal our minds, our relationships, and our hearts. However, the Bible never promises that we will be perfectly healed here on earth. This earth is a place of sin and suffering. We all suffer the consequences of the original sin in the Garden of Eden. Some physical healing only happens when God takes his people to be with him for eternity.

God does allow Storms—Jesus even let his disciples go through a massive one—but just like the biblical examples, no Storm lasts forever. The storm from Acts 27 was at least two weeks long, but even throughout it, God provided angelic answers for Paul.

We must believe that God doesn't want us in The Wilderness. He has taken his people through The Wilderness, and Jesus was driven there by the Holy Ghost. But he never intended for anyone to stay and have a permanent wilderness address.

We live in a fallen world, and God has temporarily given this world into the control of mankind. Most of the time, our pain is not from God doing something to us, but rather allowing something to happen. Our hurt and agony trouble God. He has no pleasure in the death of the wicked (Ezekiel 33:11). God says that he hears the cry of his people (Psalm 34:17).

Jesus did not tell his followers they could avoid Distresses and pain by believing in him. Quite the opposite. The apostles lost friends, family, the ability to work, sometimes their homes, and eventually their lives. All were tortured; all but one was martyred, and he was imprisoned. Bad things happen to us because we live in a sinful world. The good news is that Jesus has overcome the world (John 16:33).

*In whom are hidden all the treasures
of wisdom and knowledge.*

Colossians 2:3 (NKJV)

THE PRECIOUS JEWEL OF WISDOM

If I knew the secret of how to skip Distress, this book would be a bestseller. People would underline and highlight every word. But there is no ironclad guarantee to avoid pain and trouble in this life. The Bible has a name for the place with no pain or trouble: Heaven.

But the last verse of Psalm 107 offers a promise of understanding:

> Whoever is wise will observe these things, And they will understand the lovingkindness of the LORD. (107:43, NKJV)

"Observe" in this verse means to watch, stay awake, and pay close attention to. If we will observe these words, these stories, God's illustrations, we'll get the prize. The benefit that God offers is that we will understand the lovingkindness of the Lord. That may not sound like a desirable reward until we realize what God is saying. Understanding his lovingkindness means we acknowledge that God is good to us and that his tender mercies cover us. It's not only a powerful confidence in God's goodness; it also comes with the benefit that we'll begin to recognize his merciful hand currently at work in our lives.

It would be more exciting to offer everyone a secret recipe to avoid all Distresses, all pain. But we find something better, something *real*. God is offering an open commitment to whosoever will, that if we pay particularly close attention to this psalm, we will walk away with an understanding, a real-life grasp, of God's lovingkindness and tender mercy. What an amazing offer!

This last verse of Psalm 107 includes a special promise, a hidden gem for everyone who stays with the psalm to the very end. And the wise person will take all of this to heart. They'll be found thinking it over and paying close attention to these things. There are a few who gain wisdom from watching the lives of others around them, but most people find out what hurts by trying it themselves. There are different ways to obtain wisdom in life, but sadly many of us have to experience pain. We don't listen very well.

Despite our stubbornness and inconsistencies, God remains faithful to hear our cries and deliver us from our Distress.

Throughout Israelite history, we can see the faithful love of the Lord, even though the people often refused to listen to God's warnings. I notice the same if I review my own history. God continues to be faithful despite my failures to listen.

God will never give up on us. All around I see stories of lives that uncover the deep love that God has always had for us. We must realize throughout each Distress that God is with us every step of the way.

Oh, if everyone would realize just how much God loves us.

THE AUTHOR'S PRAYER

Dusty Wanderer: I pray that you will listen for the words of the Lord while you are in your Wilderness. God loves you, and he will rescue you. He will lead you out. He will take you on the right path and bring you to a place of connection and stability. He longs to be your Guide.

Oh, Sailor: I pray you hear these words of the Lord, even in the worst of your Storm. God loves you. He sees you in your turbulent trial, and he will bring you out. He is the Captain of your salvation, and he is with you even now.

Dear Rebel: I pray that, although you may be beaten and hurting, alone, hopeless, and bound in chains of impossibility, you know God loves you, and he will bring you out. He delights in breaking chains and destroying Prisons. He is your Deliverer.

Precious Fool: I pray that should this find you lying flat on your back, sick, and perhaps even dying in your spirit or your body, you know God's love for you. He alone can heal you. One way or another he will send a healing word to you, because he is the Healer.

This is the day, the moment when you decide to hear the voice of the Lord. Listen to these words and come back to them when the going gets tough. Hold on tightly to the Savior, your Rescuer.

He will lead you through to a better place.

I pray these words of life will bless someone's mind, soul, and body.

Don't let go of the Lord.

Whether we decide to follow Jesus or go our own way, we will all go through Distresses of one sort or another.

If I must go through some dry places, I want to be there with the Lord. If I must battle killer waves and screaming winds, I would much rather be in the middle of the Storm with Jesus than without him. Should I find myself in a Prison of my own making, or suffering the affliction of poor choices, I will humble myself and repent of my ways, trusting in his deliverance.

In all Distresses, I will cry out to him.

I will cry out.

And he will deliver.

ABOUT THE AUTHOR

SCOTT R HARPOLE

Scott Harpole is a storyteller, published author, an ever-learning student and teacher of the Word.

Scott has been sharing stories as long as he can remember, but it's his mother's Italian heritage to which he credits his insatiable quest for telling a great story. The loud and gregarious family gatherings he grew up with only served to whet his appetite for telling the most exaggerated version of whichever story was being told.

His unique perception of the insights he uncovers in the depths of The Word has been an edification to other believers for over 40 years.

Scott is known as Papa Scott to his three (soon to be four) precious grandchildren, as Dad to his four wonderful children and their spouses, and as babe to the love of his life, Jenn.

Currently living in the Midwest, Scott and Jenn now share their home with Bentley, a Great Dane.

Scott is available as a speaker or storyteller.

contact@scottharpole.com

Follow Scott to see his other books and join the Narrative Collective: www.scottharpolebooks.com

OTHER BOOKS BY SCOTT R HARPOLE

Sleepy Beach

The Giveaway Book

Hagar's Well: The God Who Sees Invisible People

COMING SOON

Name: Scott R Harpole
Title: Wanderer Sailor Rebel Fool: The God Who Rescues

Identifiers:
Library of Congress Control Number: 2025920082
ISBN: 978-0-9898512-9-9
ISBN: 978-0-9898512-8-2 eBook

Subjects: 1. Religion/General
2. Religion/Fiction

Cover Design: Ash Huttegger